'I'm here to

'I'm here to stay.

'It seems I have no choice in the matter—for now, at least.' Mollie's chin went up in a defiant gesture. 'But that doesn't mean to say I'm going to simply let you walk in and take over.'

His lips twisted in a crooked smile. 'A green-eyed spitfire like you? I don't doubt it for a minute. In fact, Mollie, I think I'm quite looking forward to doing battle with you.'

When **Joanna Neil** discovered Mills & Boon®, her life-long addiction to reading crystallised into an exciting new career writing medical romances. Her characters are probably the outcome of her varied lifestyle, which includes working as a clerk, typist, nurse and infant teacher. She enjoys dressmaking and cooking at her Leicestershire home. Her family includes a husband, son and daughter, an exuberant yellow Labrador and two slightly crazed cockatiels.

Recent titles by the same author:

TENDER LIAISON

THIS TIME FOREVER

BY
JOANNA NEIL

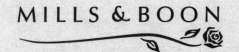

MILLS & BOON

For Niall

First published in Great Britain 2000
Harlequin Mills & Boon Limited,
Eton House, 18-24 Paradise Road, Richmond, Surrey TW9 1SR

© Joanna Neil 2000

ISBN 0 263 82235 4

Set in Times Roman 10½ on 12¼ pt.
03-0005-49167

Printed and bound in Spain
by Litografía Rosés, S.A., Barcelona

CHAPTER ONE

'WHAT on earth would possess anyone to do something like this?' Mollie muttered under her breath, sweeping a weary glance over the chaos of the surgery. Coming back to this, after a night on call, was just about enough to finish her off. The place was a mess, a scene of mindless destruction, and it made her stomach churn just to look at it.

She picked her way carefully over broken glass, wincing at the sight of precious books and equipment thrown down amongst scattered papers and over-turned furniture.

Thank heaven Uncle Robert wasn't here to see it. Her body tensed with anger at the needless, senseless rampage, and a vein in her temple began to throb painfully. Pushing her fingers distractedly through her long, unruly hair for the umpteenth time, she was troubled to find that they were shaking a little. Perhaps shock was setting in. She needed to be calm, to think clearly about things, but instead she felt like hitting out at something.

She ought to make an effort to clear up, but where to start? Pressing her knuckles against the cloth of her skirt, she pulled in a deep breath, giving herself a moment to think. The furniture? At least if she put that to rights she might begin to see a glimmer of order in things.

She seized hold of the nearest toppled chair and searched about for a clear bit of floor to stand it on.

'Should you be doing that? I'd leave it well alone, if I were you.'

Something in her chest gave an uncomfortable jerk at the intrusion, and she swung round quickly, her heart beating fast. The deep, gritty male voice sent her pulse rocketing, coming at her right out of the blue like that, and her defences were instantly up and ready, her whole body coiled for action.

She found herself staring up at a man who must have been all of six feet two, with a lean, tautly muscled frame, his long legs encased in well-cut midnight blue trousers, the breadth of his wide shoulders emphasised by the fine linen shirt he wore.

The breath escaped from her lungs in a sudden rush and she almost took a step back, but stopped herself just in time and stood her ground, fighting off a faint wave of dizziness. She was overtired and under par, but she couldn't allow herself to give in to her body's frailty, could she? She wouldn't let herself be intimidated by anyone, least of all in her own surgery.

'How did you get in here?' she demanded, her voice a little uneven.

He lifted a brow. 'The door was open,' he murmured.

Mollie couldn't decide whether he was being facetious or not. 'I thought I'd shut it,' she said with a frown. 'You almost had me jumping out of my skin, coming in on me like that.'

He made a wry grimace. 'I'm sorry if I frightene

you. There was no one in the waiting-room to answer my call, so it seemed sensible to come through here.'

His answer was reasonable enough but she was still on her guard. She could have sworn she had shut that door, but perhaps she was so tired that she couldn't trust her memory any more. Her nerves had been stretched to the limit over the last hour or so and the last thing she needed was a stranger walking in on her. How did she know he wasn't connected with what had happened here? He might have come back to search for something he had missed. A file, or something. A computer disk.

Mollie inspected him doubtfully. Admittedly, he didn't look anything like a thug. Rugged, and tough, maybe, and he would likely give someone a hard time if crossed, but he didn't have the appearance of a hardened criminal—not that she'd ever met one, but she didn't think he was a threat to her. She studied his strong-boned face, focussing on alert blue eyes and the firmly moulded mouth, her glance skimming over his crisply styled raven hair, cut neatly and attractively short. Maybe he hadn't had anything to do with this morning's happenings.

'Do I pass the test?' he drawled, his tone husky and carrying a thread of amusement. 'Or do I have to come in and start over?'

A nerve flicked in her jaw. Her mood was still brittle after the events of the day and his amusement rankled. 'Who are you?' she asked coolly, more sure of herself now. 'What are you doing here?'

He let his glance slant over her slender figure as he moved farther into the room, and she felt her fingers tighten on the chair.

He saw the slight movement and stopped. 'I hope you weren't planning on hitting me with that?' His blue eyes glittered, his tone lightly mocking her. 'The place is pretty well wrecked enough, don't you think, without adding a broken body to the scene?'

His deep, warm voice smoothed over her nerve-endings like dark chocolate, and Mollie let go of a shuddery breath she hadn't realised she had been holding. She was overreacting, wasn't she? She was so wound up that she was probably not thinking very clearly at all, and even though he was a stranger who had walked straight in off the street, his intentions might be perfectly innocent.

Slowly, she let go of the chair, getting herself under control, and said as steadily as she could, 'Didn't you see the notice on the door? There's no surgery here today. If you need to see a doctor, I'm afraid you'll have to go over to Cricklehaven.' She couldn't imagine why he would need to see a doctor, though. He was in his prime, around the early thirties, and he looked disturbingly male, strong and vital, as though his body was filled with restless energy.

'I was hoping I might see Dr Sinclair—Dr Robert Sinclair.'

Mollie shook her head. 'You can't, I'm afraid, not today. As I said, surgery's closed, and, anyway, he's ill so it's out of the question.'

He frowned. 'I'm sorry to hear that. Nothing serious, I hope?'

She gave a noncommittal shrug. 'A post-flu virus, I believe.' It was difficult to say exactly what was wrong with Uncle Robert, and the fact that it had gone on for some time and she still couldn't pin down his symptoms to anything more concrete was beginning to worry her a bit. But she wasn't about to confide that to someone she had never even met before.

He was watching her closely, his expression serious. 'Are you here in his place? It must have been upsetting for you, coming in on something like this. You weren't here when they did this, were you?'

'No, I wasn't.' She gave a small inward shudder, and braced her shoulders, looking around. 'I was out on call in the early hours this morning, and I popped in here on my way home so that I could pick up some files I needed. I arrived after the event, otherwise I might have been able to put a stop to it.'

He lifted a dark brow. 'Just as well you didn't. It could have been a risky business, especially for a woman alone. You can't tell who or what you're dealing with these days.'

She drew herself up to her full five feet four inches. 'Believe me,' she told him pithily, 'they would have been the ones to worry, not me.' It still made her angry to think that anyone had dared to wreak such mindless havoc. If she had caught them she would have set about them with the nearest object to hand, she felt sure. She had been thinking about it all morning, and the broom that was stored in the corner cupboard had played a large part in her fantasies. Mollie shook her head as if to throw them off. Her blood pressure was building up a head of steam again, and she willed herself to be calm. 'I was just about to clear the place up.'

'What about fingerprints?' His eyes narrowed on

the chair she had just put down. 'Won't the police need evidence?'

'The police have already been and gone,' she answered shortly, throwing him a brief, dismissive glance. 'I do know enough not to spoil whatever chance they have of finding who did this.' His remark had rattled her all over again. He must think she was green, wet behind the ears, and she could do without having to deal with him right now. She had enough to contend with.

Even so, she reminded herself grimly, she had to try and bear in mind that she wasn't her usual self today after what had happened, and she ought to at least make an effort to be diplomatic. So she said carefully, 'If you need directions for Cricklehaven...'

'I suppose they were looking for drugs,' he mused, unperturbed, leaning his long, well-proportioned body negligently against the filing cabinet, the one piece of furniture that remained standing. 'Youths, probably.'

'They would hardly have found any here,' she said, her voice sharp and etched with frustration. 'We're just a small rural practice, but there's a pharmacy locally, and we don't keep anything but the basics on the premises. I can't imagine what they thought they would find.'

'I don't suppose it would matter, as long as it had a market value.'

'They would have been disappointed, then.'

'And that's probably why they kicked out.' He frowned, running his glance around the room. 'What did the police say?'

Mollie pulled a face. 'They'll make enquiries.

What else can they say?' Tiredly, she rubbed the heel of her hand over her aching temple, vaguely aware that the throbbing was getting worse. Whatever the outcome, the plain fact was that she had to stay here and deal with the consequences.

Conscious that time was getting on, she bent down to scoop up an ophthalmoscope and a handful of pens and papers from the floor and then searched in vain for somewhere to put them. 'Whoever did this will be long gone by now,' she added bitterly. 'Probably headed off towards the coast to get lost in the crowd.'

'Maybe.' He straightened up, moving away from the cabinet. His gaze travelled over her assessingly, lighting on the silky, fly-away tendrils of chestnut hair that stubbornly refused to be tamed, moved on to take in the pale oval of her face, then came to rest on the soft line of her mouth. 'You look as though you've had enough for one day. You're about dead on your feet. Why don't you sit down for a while and I'll see what I can do to put the place back to rights?'

Did she look that bad? Obviously the strain was beginning to take its toll. She grimaced. Ah, well, it was nothing a good night's sleep wouldn't cure. The offer of a helping hand was tempting, but she didn't want company right now. She wanted to be on her own to sort things out, not just physically but in her mind as well.

She put the things she was holding down onto a window-ledge and said evenly, 'Thank you, it's kind of you to offer, but that really isn't necessary. It isn't your problem, and you have business to be getting on with elsewhere, don't you? Weren't you going to Cricklehaven? Didn't you need to see a doctor?'

'No, actually, I'm in fine health. It was Dr Sinclair I wanted to see, but since he's ill I'll have to arrange to meet him at some other time when he's feeling better.'

Mollie frowned. 'That could be some time away. Did you have an appointment? I'm taking over his duties for the time being, but he didn't mention to me that you were coming here.'

'I'm a few days early, in fact. We had set up a meeting for next week, but I was in the area and thought I might drop in on him.'

'You're not a patient, then? I'm sorry, I'm a bit at a loss...' She felt harassed all at once. She had prided herself on running things in an orderly fashion, but this was confusing her. With Uncle Robert out of action for the past few weeks she had needed to be especially efficient, and she had worked out a system to enable her to pull everything together. If there was anything that couldn't be dealt with straight away she made a note of it in her diary so that it could be sorted out at an opportune time, and everything had seemed to be working out reasonably well up until now.

It had been hard going, doing the work of two people, but she didn't want Uncle Robert to worry. If he thought she couldn't cope it would make him fret, and that was the last thing he needed right now. Above all, he needed rest and peace of mind.

'He normally confides in me,' she said, her brows pulling together, 'but perhaps he forgot this time. Should I know your name?'

'Sam Bradley.' He extended a hand towards her and she found her palm engulfed warmly, his long fingers curving around hers, and the sensation of tingling electricity that shot along her arm and flashed through her body was stunning, and wholly unexpected.

She swallowed hard and carefully manoeuvred her hand free. 'I'm afraid I'm still none the wiser,' she muttered huskily, trying to shake off the trembling awareness his touch had aroused in her. She was suddenly all too conscious of his latent male strength. He had an air of confidence that disconcerted her, a disturbing animal magnetism that put every one of her senses on alert. She cleared her throat. 'Perhaps you can tell me what it was that you needed to see my uncle about. Maybe I can be of help.'

'He hasn't mentioned me at all?'

Mollie shook her head, recovering now. 'Perhaps it slipped his mind.' She sent him a questioning glance, inviting him to open up, but instead of that he seemed to be preoccupied. 'Is there a problem?' she asked.

He studied her for a moment, and it bothered her that she couldn't read his expression. 'I'm sure there isn't,' he murmured, 'but, on the whole, it might be better if Dr Sinclair talked to you himself.'

Frustration made the muscles of her stomach tighten. He was keeping something back, but why? There had never been any secrets between her and Uncle Robert, and yet here was this man being totally evasive. It was thoroughly exasperating. Why couldn't he just answer a simple question?

He wasn't making any effort to go either, and she

wished that he would. Her headache was getting
worse and she wanted to be on her own so that she
could deal with it. After all that she had been through
in the last few hours the tension was building inside
her to screaming pitch, and she didn't want to have
to go on exchanging words with someone who
shouldn't even be here.

He was looking around the room, his eyes narrowed as he inspected the damage. 'This is too much
for you to handle on your own. I'll give you a hand,
sorting it out, otherwise you'll be here all day.'

He moved purposefully over to the table, which
had been pushed on its side, and lifted it back into
position as easily as if it had been made of balsa
wood. Then he righted two of the chairs, which had
once been comfortably upholstered and were now
slashed and ruined. 'These can go on one side for
later. I dare say a good upholsterer will be able to
renovate them easily enough.'

She started towards him, the beginnings of an ob-
jection framed on her lips, a frown furrowing her
brow where a tight knot was gathering inside her
head. Glass crunched under her feet, and she stared
down at the fragments.

'Careful,' he said, then asked briskly, 'Was this
the only room to be damaged, or are there others?'

'This one took the brunt of it,' she said, her tone
abstracted as she inspected the sole of her shoe. Gin-
gerly, she began to pick up pieces of broken glass,
and then she stopped, holding the pieces precariously
in her palm, wondering why on earth she was allowing the man to take over like that.

She wasn't used to having other people take control.

She had learned to be independent long ago, and it was important to her that she managed to cope in a crisis. It wouldn't do to rely on a stranger for help, and she knew nothing about this man. He still hadn't given her a proper idea of who he was, and what he was doing here.

'I can manage this well enough on my own,' she told him. 'Since my uncle isn't here to speak to you himself, I think the best thing I can do is tell him that you dropped by and get him to phone you. I'm sure you have other things you should be doing, and I'd really rather just get on with this by myself.'

He shook his head. 'I can't let you do that.'

Mollie stared at him, her mouth dropping open in surprise. 'I don't think—'

'I appreciate that you want to be alone,' he put in smoothly, 'and I can understand that it must be difficult for you to come to terms with what's happened here. You're feeling uptight, and it's only natural that you want time to yourself, but I don't think I can, in all conscience, let you stay here on your own. You look all-in. You're as white as a sheet... In fact, I'd go so far as to say that you're in a state bordering on shock.'

'I'm all right,' she told him. 'Really, I am. It was all a bit of a shock, but I'm over it now.'

'You are most certainly not all right.' He viewed her with evident scepticism, his jaw firming in a rigid, obstinate line. 'And just a short while ago you thought I might be one of the people who did this, so clearly you think whoever was responsible might come back. That isn't very likely, today at least, but I'll be here to safeguard you anyway.' He picked up a sheaf of papers and tossed them onto the table as though the matter had been decided. 'I'd suggest that you leave everything as it is and call in a firm of cleaners to sort it out, but I suspect you wouldn't do that.'

'You're right, I wouldn't.' Her green eyes sparked. 'Look, I meant what I said—you really don't need to stay. It's my problem and I can deal with it, without having to involve you.' It was second nature to her by now to try to manage things on her own. After all, if you didn't pin any expectations on other people being around to help out, no one could ever let you down. 'Thank you for the offer,' she added quietly, 'but I'll be fine.'

'I disagree.' He was totally unruffled, and very definitely, from the look of his firm, sure-footed stance, intending to stay. 'You're obviously tired out, after being on call half the night and then coming back and having to deal with this. The least I can do is to help you put things back in some kind of order.' He threw her an oblique glance.

'And then I'll drive you home because you look as though you're about at the end of your tether and I wouldn't like to see you end up having an accident through a lack of concentration or coming over faint at the wheel.' He frowned. 'Just sit down and tell me where you want things.'

'There's no need for you to worry on that score,' she said quietly. 'I can drive myself home. After all, this isn't the first time I've been overtired. In this line of work, you simply have to learn to cope.' She picked up more glass, and added drily, 'If someone calls me in the middle of the night when I'm deep asleep, I have no choice but to get up and go to work. I can hardly tell whoever it is to go and be ill some other time, when it's more convenient, can I?'

'Don't you have a locum service to call on?'

'Not at the moment but we will have. We're fairly isolated out here so the area doesn't appeal all that much to locums at the best of times, and right now the service is short-staffed.' She darted him a challenging green glance, a faint smile tugging at her lips. 'But perhaps you have an answer for that, too, Mr Bradley?'

His mouth was wry. 'I could always do the call myself. It's Dr Bradley, actually.'

'Doctor?' Mollie echoed faintly. 'You're a doctor?'

'That's what I said.'

Her mind started working overtime. A doctor...who wanted to see Uncle Robert. What was it he had said? He was a few days early?

She gnawed at the problem. 'So your meeting with my uncle has something to do with the practice? Something he hasn't confided in me?' He didn't answer, and her fingers stiffened as some of the implications rolled in on her. 'What exactly's going on here? Isn't it about time you told me the whole story?'

'I'm sure Dr Sinclair is planning to explain things to you himself—'

'But I want you to explain it to me,' she said quickly, agitation building up inside her.

His blue glance flashed over her. 'I think you should try to calm down.' His gaze shifted to her hands, and he said with a frown, 'Perhaps you had better put the glass down before—'

Exasperation flared through her, making her body tense. 'I just want you to— Ouch! Oh, oh, it hurts…'

Mollie stared down at her hand and watched the blood drip from her palm. It was a strange sight, an oddly compelling combination of bright red blood against the white of her hand, drip, drip, dripping. She watched it in a detached kind of way, until her knees began to feel peculiar, weak and shaky, and her head seemed to be filling with cotton wool.

He caught her before she fell. Strong arms folded around her, steadied her, supported her weight, and when she felt the broad expanse of his chest beneath her cheek it seemed entirely natural to rest her head in the comfortable hollow of his shoulder. It was better that way, the dizziness subsided a little when she did that, and the only sensation was one of warmth and well-being. She could feel the steady thud of his heartbeat, and it was infinitely reassuring.

'Let's get you out of here and onto a couch. Hold on.' He lifted her up and swept her out of the room and into the corridor and seemed to head unerringly for the treatment room. She knew that because her senses were slowly returning to normal, and she was beginning to feel acute dismay at the way she had snuggled into the shelter of his body and let him carry her off like that. And all for a cut hand. He must think she was a complete wimp.

He deposited her carefully on the leather couch. 'There we are. Safe and sound.' He looked into her eyes, as though trying to gauge her condition, and she responded by blinking fiercely to clear away the mist that cloaked her vision.

'I'm fine now,' she muttered. 'I don't know what came over me. I'll just go and—' She made to rise from the couch and he placed a hand on her shoulder and pushed her back down.

'You're going nowhere. Sit tight until I've had a look at that wound.' He opened a cupboard door and brought out a first-aid kit, then came and sat astride a stool next to the couch. 'Let me see.' He drew her palm towards him, then growled softly. 'Senseless. You'll need a stitch or two in that...or three or four. I'll just check to see if there's any glass left in there. Hold still.'

He switched on the lamp and arranged her hand so that he could see better. She noticed how strong his fingers were, how the backs of his hands were covered with a fine mat of hair. Odd how fingers could convey so much about a person, she mused.

He checked the wound carefully. He was gentle and thorough, and deft in his movements, trying not to hurt her, but the injury was raw and she tried not to flinch.

He glanced up at her. 'Not going to faint, are you?'

She shook her head. 'I don't think so. I hope not.'

'Good girl. I'll be as careful as I can. Once the anaesthetic works you won't feel a thing.'

She gritted her teeth. 'I know. I'm a doctor. That's what I tell my patients.' Her mouth made a pained twist. 'I'll be much more sympathetic with them from now on.'

He grinned at that, and she wished he hadn't be-cause it added yet another dimension to his bone-melting good looks, and the last thing she needed was to be sidetracked into exploring that dangerous alley. In her meagre experience, men spelled nothing but trouble and heartache, and were best left well alone.

She groaned inwardly. It was bad enough that he was still here, an hour after she had suggested that he should leave…and she still hadn't made any headway with clearing up the mess.

When he had finished tidying up her palm, she had to admit he had made a good job of it. 'Thanks,' she said, smiling up at him. 'That feels much more comfortable now.' She pulled a face. 'I'll know better than to hold onto broken glass next time.'

'I'm sure you will.' He cleared away the equipment he had used and came back to her as she was starting to get to her feet. 'No, don't try to move. Stay there for a while longer. You're still looking much too pale. I'll see if I can rustle up a cup of tea and maybe a biscuit or two.'

She moved restlessly. 'I need to get on.'

'It'll wait. Besides,' he added drily, 'you'll not be able to do much with an injured hand. It'll be tender for quite a while, I expect.'

She didn't have the strength to argue with him. He left the room, and she watched him stride away, then leaned back on the couch, feeling suddenly drained. Tea seemed like a good idea after all. With a bit of luck it might help her get a few things into perspective.

He reappeared a few minutes later, bearing a tray, complete with cups, a teapot, milk and sugar, and a selection of biscuits and flapjacks purloined from the kitchen cupboard.

'It doesn't take you long to find your way about a place, does it?' she remarked with a dry smile. 'Anyone would think you had been here for months.'

'I'm a quick learner. Drink your tea while I go and clear up—and don't waste energy objecting,' he forestalled her when she opened her mouth to speak. 'We've both been here quite long enough.'

That was certainly true. And this time it was she who had held him up, she reflected guiltily.

'Thank you for looking after me,' she said quietly. 'I'm sorry if I was abrupt with you before. All this has been upsetting for me, coming on top of a difficult night. I expect I've just been overdoing things a bit lately.'

His mouth tilted in an attractive smile. 'I realise that, and it's all right. Just you sit there and rest for a while.'

He went off, taking his tea with him, and she swallowed the remains of hers and polished off a few biscuits, belatedly remembering that she had missed out on a meal or two with all the upset today. No wonder she was feeling drained. The small snack helped fill her energy gap, and gave her the lift she needed.

A few minutes later, feeling more like her old self, she went to join him in the surgery and set about putting things into some kind of order as best she could with one hand out of action. Sam Bradley made to stop her, but she quelled him with a determined frown that brooked no argument, and he let her get on with it.

It didn't take as long as she had feared, not with
two of them working, and he seemed to have enough
energy for both of them.

'I found some bin liners in the kitchen,' he remarked. 'All the stuff that's beyond repair can go out
for the refuse collection. As to the rest, it probably
looks worse than it really is. The bulk of the paperwork is still intact in the folders, and I dare say the
rest can be sorted reasonably well, given time. Let-
ters, and hospital reports and suchlike, at least have
addresses and names on them.'

'With luck, most of the information will be held
on computer. It's only the more recent correspon-
dence that will need checking, as that won't have
been logged yet.' Mollie looked around and heaved
a sigh. 'I think that's about all we can do for now.'

She gave him a brief but warm smile. 'Thanks for
all your help. It would have taken me much longer
on my own, and I do appreciate it. I'm sorry you've
had such a waste of an afternoon.'

'That's OK. I was glad to be able to do something.' His mouth tilted in a way that melted her
insides, and she tried hard to ignore the sensation.

'Perhaps I'll see you again some time, in better
circumstances…' she murmured. 'Maybe when you
have your meeting with my uncle.' She had given up
trying to prise information out of him on that score.
She would tackle Uncle Robert about it later.

'You haven't quite got rid of me yet, you know,'
he answered drily. 'I did say that I would drive you
home.'

She shook her head. 'I've kept you far too long

already. I'll be fine now. I plan to go home and relax in the bath and then catch up on some sleep.'

'With that hand you'll be a danger on the road.' He fished his car keys out of a pocket. 'Come on, I'll see that you get back safely.'

She made a last effort to resist. 'My car—'

'I'll make arrangements for it to be picked up.' He opened the door and waved her through. 'All you need to do is to give me the directions to your house.'

Mollie gave up trying to be independent. Her head was pounding, her hand was stinging and she was really in no shape to argue. She hated having to rely on anyone for anything, but it seemed she really had no choice this time.

Perhaps, once she reached home he would take his leave of her and be on his way, and then she might begin to relax a little. She could only hope…

CHAPTER TWO

'IT'S only three or four miles to the cottage,' Mollie told Sam Bradley as she settled herself in the passenger seat of his car.

Her jacket snagged beneath her and she shifted to tug it free. As she moved, her knee made contact with the warmth of his hand just as he reached for the gear lever, and the breath caught in her throat, checked by the sudden rush of sensation that surged unexpectedly through her. It was just a fleeting touch, because she quickly swung her legs to one side, but her body was already quivering in response to that brief touch and her cheeks flushed with heat.

She hoped he hadn't noticed her reaction, and when she glanced up at him his face gave nothing at all away, except that she thought there might have been the slightest twist to his mouth. That could have been her imagination working overtime, though.

'I'll need directions to your place,' he prompted, and she hurriedly pulled her mind back to order.

'Turn left at the Wheatsheaf Inn, and drive along the lane for a couple of miles. It's the first stone-built cottage you'll come to,' she managed evenly. 'It's set back off the road a bit, but I don't think you'll miss it. There's a mass of honeysuckle covering the garden wall, and a climbing rose on a trellis at the gateway.'

It was roomy inside the car, she discovered once

she allowed herself to relax, and it was a pleasure to
sink into the comfortable upholstery. The engine
purred smoothly as they passed through the
Yorkshire countryside, and after a while her senses
were lulled in a way that meant she had to struggle
not to close her eyes. Outside, the afternoon sun was
still hot, but the darkened windows shielded its fierce
rays.

'Does your uncle live close by as well?' Sam
Bradley's gravel-tinged voice broke into her
thoughts.

'We live in the same house, have done for a number of years now.'

'That must be handy, with both of you working in
the practice.' He sent her a sidelong glance. 'You
didn't get around to telling me your name.'

'Mollie Sinclair.'

'So, Dr Sinclair must be your father's brother?'

'That's right.'

She didn't volunteer any further information, and
he commented lightly, 'Having the same surname
must cause problems in surgery, I imagine. How do
you get round it?'

She made a wry face. 'I'm generally known as Dr
Mollie. He's Dr Sinclair.'

Sam grinned. 'Sounds like a reasonable solution.'
He turned off the main road at the pub as she had
directed, and after a few minutes murmured, 'This
looks like it. I see what you mean about the flowers.
It's a riot of colour, isn't it? Who does the garden-
ing?'

'Both of us when we have the time, but lately
we've had a man from the village come over for a

couple of hours a week just to tidy things up a bit.
It's quite a large garden, and it takes some work to
keep it looking good. Unfortunately, with my uncle
being ill, he hasn't been able to do much, and I
haven't had as much time as I would have liked to
keep on top of it.'

'I can imagine it would be difficult.' He drew the
car to a halt on the driveway in front of the house.

Mollie hesitated, wondering whether, out of po-
liteness, she ought to invite him in. Her tired bones
urged her to wave him on his way, but in the end
her conscience got the better of her. It was the least
she could do after he had spent the afternoon helping
her out. She said slowly, 'Would you like to come
in for a cup of something?'

His blue eyes assessed her. 'I wouldn't want to put
you to any trouble. You've had a difficult day.'

'It's no—'

'Mollie—is that you?' Uncle Robert's voice broke
into their conversation, and she looked up to see the
older man coming slowly and awkwardly along the
path towards them.

He looked frail and thin, his tall figure slightly
bent, his dear face pulled into the now familiar lines
of pain which he tried to hide from her. Mollie
watched him, her teeth tugging awkwardly at her
lower lip. If only she could get to the bottom of what
was wrong with him.

She opened the car door and stepped out to greet
him, giving him a warm hug. She registered the thin-
ness of his frame with a faint sense of shock. He was
wearing a fine cotton shirt, and she could feel the
bony, wasted limbs that up to now had been hidden

beneath a sweater. He had been losing weight over the last few weeks, but it had clearly reached a point where something had to be done.

'Your hand!' he exclaimed, distracting her as he saw the bandage for the first time. 'What have you done to yourself? I've been worried about you. When you were late getting back I wondered if you were still out on call...whether something had gone wrong...'

'Everything's fine,' she began, trying to soothe him, but he had turned to look at the car.

'Where's your car? You haven't been in an accident, have you? Who's this with you?'

Sam climbed out of the car and came towards him, and Mollie could see that Uncle Robert quickly recognised him. 'Dr Bradley...Sam...it's good to see you again—but what's been going on? Is someone going to enlighten me?'

'I just had a small accident with some glass,' Mollie explained, 'and Dr Bradley was kind enough to drive me home.'

'You must come in,' her uncle said, gesturing to Sam to go into the house with them. 'I'll put the kettle on, and you can tell me all about it.'

They went through to the kitchen, Robert following more slowly. He stopped at the table and put his hand on the back of a chair, leaning against it for support.

'Sit down while I see to the tea,' Mollie suggested quickly, going over to the sink to fill the kettle. When he would have put up an argument she went on, 'I can manage perfectly well with this.' She held up her good hand and added, 'You're supposed to be resting. You make yourself comfortable and talk to Dr Bradley while I get on.'

'I want to know how you came to hurt yourself…and how you two came to be together.'

'There was a break-in at the surgery—' At his shocked exclamation she hurried on, 'But it's been dealt with, and everything's under control now. Dr Bradley just happened along this afternoon, and he helped me to tidy up.'

'But you could have been in danger,' he said fretfully. 'Anything might have happened—'

'No, no…nothing happened. I was perfectly safe.'

Sam was standing by the door, and she felt his eyes narrow on her. She lifted her chin, busying herself with putting out cups and saucers. He hadn't said anything for the last minute or two, letting them get on with it, but she had been constantly aware of him. While they talked he had been taking careful note of his surroundings, slowly pacing the room, and she couldn't help thinking that he reminded her of a lion on the prowl. The image disturbed her. It sent her nervous system into overdrive and left her feeling thoroughly flustered.

'Have a chair and sit down, won't you?' she suggested, using a brisk tone to cover her confusion. She poured hot water from the kettle into the teapot. 'Perhaps you can tell my uncle all about it while I go and freshen up.'

'Yes, please, do that,' Robert said quickly, motioning Sam to a chair opposite. 'It was a good thing you managed to get over here ahead of time. You will stay and have dinner with us, won't you?'

Ahead of time. Mollie's shoulders stiffened a fraction. There were a lot of questions she wanted answered regarding that, but this was not the moment, with Uncle Robert looking so weary and distracted, and she bit them back. Instead, she gave Sam a warning look and said, 'You will make sure you won't tire him?'

Cool blue eyes met hers. 'I believe you can rely on me to know how to behave.'

Mollie gritted her teeth on the silent reproof, and laid a hand on her uncle's shoulder. 'Give me a few minutes to myself and then I'll fix us something to eat.'

She left the tea tray on the table in front of them and escaped upstairs. Maybe, when she came back down again, one or other of them would tell her the bits of the story that she didn't know…like why Sam was here in the first place.

She took time to have a quick bath, a fairly difficult manoeuvre, having to keep her injured hand out of the way, but at least she felt better for the effort. Dressing was another problem, but she managed to ease on a skirt and top and pull a brush through her hair. At least she felt a bit more energised now, and a fraction more inclined to do battle with pots and pans and the hob. More to the point, she might be better able to deal with Sam.

When she went downstairs, though, she was startled to be met by tantalising smells coming from the kitchen, and she sniffed the air, trying to work out what was cooking. More to the point, who was doing the cooking, and why? It had better not be Uncle Robert, he simply wasn't up to it. She frowned, and quickened her step.

'Feeling better?' Sam took the wind out of her sails, slanting a disconcertingly thorough glance over her as she walked into the kitchen. As his gaze wandered over her, she wondered distractedly if the ribbed top she was wearing clung perhaps a little too closely to her curves, and whether she ought to have opted for a flared skirt instead of this classically tapered one. It was too late now, though, to go and change.

A gleam of approval sparkled in his eyes. 'Taking the time to freshen up seems to have done you some good. At least there's more colour in your cheeks now.'

'I'm fine.' Mollie quickly averted her gaze from that unnerving scrutiny and moved over to the table. She stared down at a number of foil packages. 'What's all this?'

'We decided it would be easier on you if I went down to the local take-away and brought in some food,' Sam explained, coming to stand beside her. 'There's a fairly wide selection here, so I hope you'll find something you fancy.'

'I'm sure I will.' It was thoughtful of him to provide food for them, and the appetising smells coming from the packages were making her mouth water. She hadn't eaten anything but a few biscuits all day, and her stomach was telling her that she was ravenous.

'Good.' His disarming smile made her pulse leap, and the brush of his long, tautly muscled body against hers made her suddenly flustered.

'I'll warm some plates,' she muttered, moving over to the cooker and putting some distance between them. 'Why don't you go into the dining-room, and I'll bring everything through?'

He was beginning to make the kitchen look small and overcrowded, and she realised that she was far too conscious of him. She was only a head shorter than he, yet he seemed to tower over her. He was powerfully built, his tall frame vibrating sheer male energy, and her senses swirled in chaotic disorder, just having him near.

Her throat closed in a small spasm as she felt his shrewd gaze resting on her. She doubted those eyes missed much. 'You'll be more comfortable in there,' she muttered diffidently, 'there's more room.' She indicated the glass doors to one side of the kitchen.

'As you like.' His mouth twisted in sardonic amusement. 'But I think I'd better give you a hand, seeing that your stitches are still so recent.'

'How on earth am I going to manage when you're not here?' she countered drily, sliding plates into the oven.

'That reminds me,' Robert put in, oblivious to the undercurrents flowing around him. 'Where are you staying, Sam? Are you back at your parents' house?'

Sam shook his head. 'They're away at the moment.' He found a tray on the worktop and began piling the packages onto it. 'They weren't expecting me to come down here for another week, so they invited some friends over to house-sit for them.'

'So, do you have a place to stay? Didn't you say you were looking to buy a place round here?'

'I've found one—a decent-sized property down by the river—and I'm really pleased to have signed the deal, but it needs a few things done to it before I can move in. The builders are there right now, putting in a new kitchen and adding a shower room to the master bedroom. In the meantime, I've booked a room at the Blue Bell Inn.'

Robert looked concerned. 'Give them a ring and tell them you won't be needing it any longer. We can't have you staying there, not when there's a room going spare here. My daughter Laura's room has been standing empty since she moved out. You can have that. Besides, it will make things much simpler all round in the short-term while you're finding your feet.'

Mollie was stunned. Sam Bradley, staying here? How would she cope? Her nerves had been jumping all over the place after she had spent just a few hours with him this afternoon, and it wasn't all down to the break-in. Why on earth was Uncle Robert thinking of letting him get involved in their lives like this? What was going on?

She opened her mouth to say something, but Robert started to get up from his chair just then and swayed slightly.

Sam was nearest and put a hand out to steady him. 'Here, let me help you into the other room,' he said quietly. 'Perhaps some food will make you feel a bit perkier, too.'

'I must have stood up too quickly, that's all. Made me a bit light-headed for a moment. I'm fine now.' Robert gently shrugged off the hand and made his way slowly and independently towards the dining-room. Sam watched him go, his expression thoughtful.

'It's sheer pride,' Mollie said under her breath. 'H

refuses to admit that he can't manage, but he's getting worse, little by little. His blood pressure's low, and it seems to me he's losing weight.'

'He looks as though he's in some pain.'

'Yes, he's mentioned some vague abdominal symptoms, but we haven't been able to pin down the cause as yet. So far, none of the tests have been conclusive. A lot of his symptoms are non-specific, and that makes it all the more difficult to diagnose. He's seen someone at the hospital, but all he came up with was some kind of virus, or fatigue syndrome. I have to admit, I'm getting worried about him.'

'I can imagine you must be. Can't you refer him to someone else for a second opinion?'

'I have done, but the consultant's on holiday for the next week or so and that means we have to wait a little longer before he can see him.'

She bit back a sigh and took the plates from the oven, leaving Sam to pick up the tray and carry it through to the dining-room. Maybe after some food and a good night's sleep she would be able to think more clearly and come up with an answer to the problem herself. Just lately she had been too weary from overwork to do anything more than flop out at the end of the day.

They sat down to eat, and she was glad she hadn't had to go to the trouble of cooking. She could even put aside the questions she wanted answered until she had eaten her fill. The food was delicious, tender meat and succulent vegetables and wholesome rice with prawns, sweetcorn and peppers, and she savoured each mouthful until at last she felt replete.

She noticed, though, that her uncle hadn't eaten much.

'Aren't you very hungry?' she asked, and he shook his head.

'I'm just a little weary,' he said. 'I keep hoping that all this rest will bring me back on form again, but it seems to be taking a while. I'm sorry, my dear. I feel that I've let you down, leaving you to cope with everything these last few weeks.'

'Of course you haven't let me down,' Mollie exclaimed, reaching out to touch his hand. 'How can you think such a thing? You're not well, and you need to get your strength back. You mustn't worry about me, I'm doing just fine. The practice is running smoothly, and there's nothing I can't handle on my own. All you have to do is concentrate on getting well.'

'I know you're managing everything on your own, but you shouldn't have to.' He moistened his lips a little, his manner hesitant. He looked uncomfortable.

Mollie pushed her plate away, then picked up a serviette and wiped her fingers. 'It's all right, believe me. You don't have any reason to feel concerned.'

He shook his head. 'It isn't. Not really. That's why I spoke to Sam, here. I wanted to do right by you.' He appeared to be ill at ease for a moment. 'You must understand I know how hard you've had to work these last few weeks, and I couldn't sit back any longer and let you do it. That's why I asked Sam to join us.'

Mollie's fingers closed spasmodically on the serviette. 'Join us? What do you mean? You can' mean—'

'I've asked Sam to come and work with us at the practice,' he said flatly. 'I heard good things about him from some friends of mine, and I know he'll be a godsend to us. It was just fortunate that he was looking to move back to Yorkshire at this point in time— No, wait, hear me out,' he urged her when she would have interrupted. 'I'm not getting any younger, and even with my full health and strength I'd want to be thinking of cutting down on my hours. So it makes sense to think ahead. Sam's ideal for the practice…you'll see.'

Mollie felt as though the breath had been knocked out of her. 'But you didn't say a word of this to me,' she said, her mind reeling in shock. 'You kept it from me, and simply went ahead on your own. How could you do that? You've never done anything like that before—we've always shared in the decision-making—'

'I know, I know…but, you see, I knew you wouldn't hear of it. You would have put obstacles in the way because you wouldn't want me to think you couldn't cope, or because the practice couldn't afford to take on another doctor. It had to be done, though. It was no use trying to kid myself any longer. I thought I could get back on my feet quickly, but in the end I've had to admit that it isn't going to be that easy.'

She said unhappily, 'You're right, I would have objected. I am objecting.' She frowned at Sam, then looked back at her uncle. 'Don't you understand how I feel? I didn't even have any say in who was taken on, and yet I'm expected to work alongside him. Don't you see how unfair that is?' She stared at him in bewilderment. 'Besides, if there had to be another doctor—and I'm disputing that—perhaps a woman doctor would have fitted in better, given the rising number of pregnancies in the area and the number of children who need to be looked after.'

Sam's blue glance flicked sharply over her. 'Do you think I have no knowledge of obstetrics or paediatrics? I would hardly be in general practice if I couldn't deal competently with either one.'

'You're looking at it from the doctor's point of view,' she retorted sharply. 'What about the patient?'

'I'm sure that if a small minority objected to having a male doctor oversee their care, they would sign up on your list. I'm equally sure that it would be a minority.' His mouth twisted grimly. 'Let's get down to the nitty-gritty of it, shall we? The real issue at stake here is your insistence on wanting to cope alone. That's totally unnecessary and, frankly, it's extremely foolhardy. You said yourself that you may be called out at night and then have to work the next day. You can hardly be expected to give your best to your patients in those circumstances.'

Her eyes flashed with indignation. 'There is never a time when my patients receive less than the best,' she flared hotly.

'How would you know? If you're constantly tired, you're hardly likely to be a fit judge of that.'

She stiffened. 'Since you only arrived here today, I don't think you're in a position to make any judgement on how I do my job.'

Robert struggled to his feet, acutely distressed. 'Mollie, please, Dr Bradley is a guest in our house.'

Mollie pulled in a deep breath. 'I'm sorry, Uncle.

You're right, of course.' She turned to Sam and said huskily, 'My apologies. This is upsetting for my uncle, and I should have known better.'

Sam's eyes glinted narrowly, and she suspected he knew full well that she was not the least bit contrite. Robert, though, seemed satisfied.

'I know I shouldn't have dropped this on you without warning,' he said. 'It's just that I wasn't sure if Sam would accept, and I didn't want to stir the waters unnecessarily, especially as you already had enough on your plate. I did it for the best of reasons, believe me, and I'm sure if you take time to think it through you'll come to understand the situation.'

He paused to take a breath, and Mollie was distressed to see that he looked pale and haggard. 'Sam has agreed to stay for six months at least,' he went on, 'with a view to a partnership after that. I would really like you and him to get on well together. It would help such a lot towards the smooth running of the practice, and I should be much easier in my mind.' He seemed to falter then, and sat down again, worn out by the small exertion.

Mollie went over to him and smoothed a hand gently over his shoulder. 'You mustn't worry. I'm sure things will work out, and you'll be back on your feet in no time at all. Is there anything I can get you? Are you in pain?'

'No, no. I shall be fine now. Just knowing that Sam is here to take some of the load off your shoulders is enough to make me feel better.' He smiled wearily and patted her hand. 'I think I might have an early night though.' He turned to look at Sam and said regretfully, 'I'm sorry to have to leave you like this... There's so much we need to talk about, but—'

Sam waved away his apology. 'That's all right, I understand. You go and try to get some rest. There'll be plenty of time for us to talk in the morning.'

Mollie readied herself to help her uncle up to bed. Glancing back towards Sam, she said briefly, 'I'll show you which is to be your room, if you like.'

'Thank you.'

He followed them up the stairs and waited while she saw Robert into a bedroom at the far end of the corridor. She switched on the reading lamp in there and plumped up the pillows on his bed, before saying goodnight and adding, 'Give me a shout if you need anything in the night. God bless.' Then, giving him a light kiss on the cheek, she left the room.

Sam was waiting on the landing, leaning negligently against the stair rail. He straightened as she approached. 'What happens if he's ill in the night? Will you hear him if he calls you?'

'There's an intercom he can use to bleep me and, anyway, my room's right next to his so there isn't usually a problem. Yours is across the landing, just here, and the bathroom is alongside.' She opened the door to the bathroom and showed him the pleasantly tiled interior with its pale apricot-coloured suite and plush carpet. 'Help yourself to anything you need in there. There should be plenty of towels in the airing cupboard. I'll get you some fresh sheets and make up the bed for you.'

'I can do that for myself.'

'If that's what you'd prefer...' A thought struck her. 'You don't appear to have any luggage with you

If you…um…' She hesitated, feeling slightly flustered. 'If you need a pair of pyjamas or anything, I
could probably find you some of Uncle Robert's…'

'That's OK, you don't need to worry about that.
I'll do perfectly well in the raw. It's still late summer
so I'm hardly likely to freeze.' He grinned at her,
and she felt her cheeks suddenly heat at the image
of finely honed musculature and nakedness his words
conveyed. She mentally batted the provocative vision
fiercely away. That was something she most definitely did not want to dwell on. It was quite bad
enough that he was here in the first place, without
having him disturb her subconscious as well.

'Yes, well…if that's how you feel…' Her voice
tailed off and, feeling hot and bothered, she busied
herself fetching linen from the cupboard. She sensed
his amusement and had to give herself a mental
shake. Wretched man. She couldn't let him see that
she was affected by him in any way. Crossly, she
marched into his room and dropped the sheets onto
the bed.

He observed her thoughtfully through narrowed
eyes. 'It may not turn out to be as bad as you imagine.'

She blinked. 'What do you mean?'

'Me being around. You might even come to appreciate having me on hand as a back-up.'

'I don't need a back-up,' she said patiently. 'With
luck, Uncle Robert will be on form again before too
long, and we could go on as before.' She grimaced
and corrected herself. 'We could have if he hadn't
thought it necessary to bring you in. There was no
need. I have everything well organised and under

control, and things have been running smoothly enough.'

'Until now,' he pointed out with dry scepticism. 'You've been worked off your feet. Besides, things didn't look to be going so well this afternoon.'

'That was something quite out of the ordinary—'

'But it could happen again. What if there's another break-in and you're on the premises when it happens? You were lucky this time, but next time you might not be.'

'Then I'll have to be prepared for it.'

He shook his head, his mouth making a wry shape. 'As it is, you're an easy target, a woman alone. At least my presence might serve as a deterrent.'

'You're planning on being around for every second, are you?' she said tersely.

'I'll be there in the evenings when the surgery is more vulnerable,' he responded smoothly. 'In any case, after what I saw today, I'll be looking into installing some safety measures. Alarm systems, panic buttons and the like.'

Mollie's eyes flashed. 'Will you? You've only been here five minutes, and already you're making decisions off the top of your head. It isn't as simple as snapping your fingers and assuming that everything can be put right, you know. There are other things to take into consideration—like finance, for example.'

His mouth tightened. 'Listen to me, Mollie…' She would have turned away, but he took hold of her shoulders, his hands closing gently but firmly around her upper arms, and he drew her back to face him. 'Come down off that high horse and face facts.

know you don't want a new partner, but you have to go along with this for your uncle's sake. At least you can try to reconcile yourself to the fact that I can take some of the burden off you.'

Mollie's jaw set. He wouldn't be satisfied with simply helping out. He was too strong-minded for that, too confident and assertive. 'You're an outsider,' she muttered, 'but you think you have all the answers, don't you? It doesn't work like that. Things don't come that easily, or we'd have fixed everything ourselves.' She tried to break out of his grasp, but he wasn't letting her go.

His mouth firmed, edged with impatience. 'I never said I had all the answers, and I'm not some stranger to the area. I've lived here for a good part of my youth and I know the territory. I'm not a threat to you.'

'Aren't you?' She wished she could believe that, but she saw the fierce glitter of determination that sparked in the depths of his blue eyes, and knew that he was not a man to give up a fight. She felt the warmth from his long fingers as they lightly pressed her tender flesh, sensed the faint, pleasing fragrance of musk that mingled with his own male scent and fought against the feminine weakness of her body which made her undeniably vulnerable.

'I'm here to help. I'm here to stay. Accept it.'

'I know you're going to be around,' she muttered. There was nothing she could do about it yet, but that didn't mean she couldn't persuade her uncle to change things once he was well again, did it? She had grown used to the way things were, just her and Uncle Robert, rubbing along together smoothly. Just the thought of having all that thrown out of balance made her edgy.

She had to be a realist, though. 'It seems I have no choice in the matter—for now at least.' Her chin went up in a defiant gesture. 'But that doesn't mean to say I'm going to simply let you walk in and take over.'

His lips twisted in a crooked smile. 'A green-eyed spitfire like you? I don't doubt it for a minute.' Slowly, he released her. 'In fact, Mollie, I think I'm quite looking forward to doing battle with you.'

CHAPTER THREE

IT WAS a crunching sound that woke her. Mollie rubbed her eyes and tried to surface from the fog of sleep, struggling to focus her mind on what it was. Then there was a faint clunk and more crunching, less noisy and more even-paced this time, like someone walking along a gravelled path.

Sunlight filtered through the curtains, and she blinked. A car, that was what she had heard. Someone was calling at the house and here she was, still in bed. She reached for her watch from the bedside table and sucked in her breath when she saw that it was the middle of the morning. How could she have slept for so long?

A quick glance out of the window made her frown. It was Sam's car on the drive so he must have been out and come back in again.

She hurriedly washed and dressed, tugging on hip-hugging jeans and a cream-coloured T-shirt, and then took a moment or two to pull a brush through her hair. As usual it refused to do what she wanted, tumbling this way and that in a riot of waves, and she pulled a face and gave up on it. She was late enough already.

Sam was making coffee when she went into the kitchen a few minutes later. He had his back to her, but that did nothing to diminish the impact of his long lean figure and the broad sweep of his shoulders. Mollie felt a surge of all kinds of conflicting emotions which were best left buried. She didn't want him in the house at all. He was simply too intensely male and altogether far too disturbing to have around. She was used to quiet, undemanding Sundays at home, when she could relax and please herself, but relaxation looked like it was totally out of reach now. His mere presence made her jumpy.

He turned and looked her way, his gaze steadily meeting hers, a faint smile pulling at the edges of his mouth. 'Hello, there. I don't need to ask if you feel better for a good night's sleep. You look positively vibrant.'

She blinked in response, shifting uneasily at the thought that she might have been caught staring. 'Do I?' Perhaps it was just as well he couldn't read her mind.

He nodded, his glance shifting reluctantly from the tumbled, silky mass of her hair to roam in lazy appreciation over the gentle curves of her slender figure, seeming to leave a searing trail of flame in its wake. 'And a few more other things besides, but I think those might be best kept to myself till I know you better.' His devilish smile unsettled her, and she blinked again, a flood of heat washing along her cheek bones. 'Want some coffee?' he murmured.

He lifted the coffee pot, and the mundane action quickly brought her back to her senses. He had been teasing her, that was all, and she was annoyed with herself for allowing him to throw her off balance. 'Thanks,' she muttered. 'I could do with some.'

He filled two mugs with the hot liquid and handed her one. She sipped gratefully, studying him surreptitiously from under her lashes. He was wearing immaculate grey trousers and a dark blue shirt, and she could see that he was in perfect shape, firmly muscled and flat-stomached, definitely too much to take in first thing in the morning. Except that it wasn't first thing. It was horrendously late. She gulped down more coffee. It was high time she pulled herself together.

Sam's long fingers curved around his mug and he lifted it to his lips. She noticed that his jaw was tinged with a blue-grey shadow which hadn't been there before. It lent him a faintly roguish air, and added to his rugged attraction in a way that made her swallow hard. Her glance lifted and she discovered to her dismay that he was watching her in turn, his eyes holding a gleam that was disturbingly feral. He knew full well that his presence here was spiking her nerves. Her warning system flashed onto red alert. She had better keep her wits about her where he was concerned. He was trouble, no doubt about it.

'You look as though you've had a hard night,' Mollie commented starkly. 'Have you been out on the town?' That must have been a long round trip, since the nearest night life was around twenty miles away. Still, perhaps he needed the stimulation. She scowled into her coffee.

'There were a couple of call-outs, one in the early hours of the morning and then another around seven.' He put his mug down and ruefully stroked a hand along his jaw. 'I guess I need a shave.'

'Call-outs?' The casually imparted information

caught her unawares. 'But I didn't know about them. I didn't hear anything.'

'I picked the phone up as soon as it rang. I didn't want to disturb you.'

'But you should have woken me,' she said quickly, pushing her mug down on to the worktop and looking up at him, her eyes wide with dismay.

His lips twisted derisively. 'The whole point of the exercise was to make sure that both you and your uncle had a restful night.'

'But I was supposed to be on call last night. We could hardly expect you to start work as soon as you arrived here.'

He shrugged. 'I didn't mind. I had a word with Robert about it and he agreed that I could make a start. You've had enough to contend with recently, and this way at least you get to have a Sunday off. You'll be back at the surgery soon enough tomorrow.'

'That was thoughtful of you,' she said quietly. 'I was glad of a lie-in, even if it does seem horrendously late now.' She pulled a face, then added on a firmer note, 'But from now on I think we should draw up a rota and stick to it…and we should all be in on any decision-making and kept aware of any changes to the status quo. There are a number of things I want to—'

'What you need,' he cut in smoothly, 'is breakfast. No more talk of work, but a good, hot meal instead It'll set you up for the day, you mark my words.'

'Breakfast?' Her brows lifted in sharp frustration 'Don't you mean lunch?' She shot a despairing glance at the clock on the wall. 'How could I hav slept for so long? And what about Uncle Robert? I haven't even spoken to him yet this morning.'

'He seems to be all right. I saw him earlier, and he told me that a friend was coming by to take him out by the river for an hour or so. They must have gone while I was out. It'll do him good to get out into the fresh air.'

'I suppose it will.' His mention of breakfast had woken up her stomach and she began to hunt in the cupboard for a frying pan. 'Have you eaten yet?' She doubted it as he had been out on call for most of the morning, and he was probably starving.

He shook his head. 'There wasn't time. The second call was to an asthmatic child on the Mulberry Estate, and it sounded pretty serious.'

She flicked him a concerned glance. 'The Simmons boy? About five years old?'

'That's the one.'

'What happened? Is he all right?'

'He'll be OK. I gave him oxygen, then nebulised salbutamol and intravenous hydrocortisone. He was stable when I left, and I didn't feel it was necessary to hospitalise him. It can be upsetting for children if we have to do that, and if the asthma can be managed in the home I think that's for the best.'

'Do you have any idea what brought it on?'

'It may be that he hasn't been using his inhaler properly. We'll have to monitor that. Do you run a clinic?'

'Once a month for asthma patients. There aren't too many on the list, but Lee's parents don't always turn up for his appointments. There have been problems with shift-working and so on.'

'That's something we must follow up, then. Also, I suspect his condition isn't being helped by the atmosphere he's having to breathe in. Both parents smoke, and I've pointed out to them that his lungs can't cope with that. If they can't give it up, the least they can do is smoke outside the house, out of Lee's way, and install a fan in the kitchen.'

She could imagine Sam speaking his mind. Even in telling her about it there was a controlled anger in his expression, and she wondered if he might have gone too far. The doctor–patient relationship sometimes trod a fine line. 'How did they take that?'

His mouth made a rueful twist. 'They seemed a bit subdued after I had sounded off at them. Wrong of me to get worked up, I suppose, but the incident made me angry. Their child was put in a life-threatening situation, and it will happen again unless they start to take his condition seriously.' A muscle strained in his jaw. 'I believe they will from now on.'

'He's never had a really nasty episode before this. I expect it has come as a shock.'

'One that will have taught them a lesson, I hope.'

Mollie muttered agreement, then opened the fridge door and peered inside. 'Bacon and eggs?' she queried.

'Sounds good to me.' He pulled a loaf from the bread bin and searched for the bread board.

'What was the other call?' She busied herself at the hob while he began to cut thick slices of bread.

'A young boy with a stomach bug. Richard Lansdowne…twelve years old?' He lifted a brow in query, and she nodded.

'I know the family. There's an older brother, about sixteen, and a new baby. The father of the two older boys moved out some time ago but there's a new man on the scene these days, I think.' She sliced tomatoes and dropped them into the pan alongside the bacon.

'I thought the mother looked worn out.'

'She has a lot on her plate, I imagine. What kind of stomach bug was it? Anything to be concerned about?'

'Gastroenteritis, caused by something he'd eaten, I think. I've advised the mother that he should stay in bed and drink plenty of fluids and have nothing to eat for twenty-four hours. If his condition doesn't improve she'll give us a ring, but I see no reason why he shouldn't be back on his feet before too long.' He sniffed the air approvingly and looked in the direction of the hob. 'That smells good.'

They ate at the table in the kitchen, not saying much except for a comment or two about the local area, and Sam mentioned he had seen to it that her car had been returned. He had also been to fetch his suitcases from the pub where he had booked a room.

Robert came in as they were finishing the meal, and she noticed unhappily that there was a pinched look about him. The change of scene might have lifted his spirits, but he wasn't looking any better for it. He was holding a carrier bag and he looked around for a place to put it.

'Did you have a good time? Did you go fishing?' Mollie asked.

'Jim fished. I just watched and helped him eat his sandwiches. He sent these tomatoes for you. Home-grown in his greenhouse.' He made to hand her the bag and it slipped from his fingers. 'Sorry…I just need to sit down.' He moved over to a chair and collapsed weakly against it.

Mollie looked at him anxiously. 'Are you feeling dizzy?'

'Legs aren't what they were. I'll be OK in a minute.'

She hurried over to him and took hold of his arm. 'Let me help you into the other room. You'll be better off in an armchair.'

Carefully, she walked with him into the living-room and then supported him while he lowered himself into his seat.

'You know,' she murmured, 'I really think we should do more tests and try to get to the bottom of what's wrong.'

He waved the suggestion away. 'There's no need for more tests. I've been through all that at the hospital. It's just a virus, and now on top of that I'm coming down with a cold, that's all. It's making me feel a bit groggy.'

Mollie shook her head. 'I'm not satisfied that there isn't more we can do. I think we need to test your blood-sugar levels for a start, and I want to look into the possibility of a type of anaemia being one of your problems. A urine test might be a good idea as well.'

'It's all a lot of fuss about nothing. I can't be bothered with any of it.'

'Even so, try to bear with me for a little while, will you?' she said coaxingly. 'Just to please me. After all, no harm can come of looking into one or two more possibilities while we wait for the consultant to get back to work, can it?'

He sighed and rested his head against the back of his chair. 'If you must. You'll not let up until I give in, will you?'

Her mouth quirked. 'You know me so well, don't you? But I only want what's best. Stay there and rest while I go and finish up in the kitchen.'

He nodded, closing his eyes, and she watched him for a moment, disturbed by his unhealthy pallor. There had to be a way of finding out what was wrong with him, even if it meant a slow process of eliminating the various possibilities one by one.

When she went back into the kitchen she saw that Sam had rescued the tomatoes from the floor and was putting them into a bowl.

He sent her an oblique glance. 'Is he more comfortable now?'

She nodded. 'I think so.' She began to stack crockery into the dishwasher.

'You're very fond of him, aren't you?'

'Yes, I am. He's been like a father to me. He's taken care of me for such a long time.'

'What about your own parents?'

'I lost them when I was about twelve years old.' Her mouth wavered a fraction. 'My father had an accident when he was on a climbing holiday in Scotland, and my mother took it very badly. She seemed to lose interest in things and didn't look after herself. She was always frail, short and very slender. After the accident she didn't eat properly and she wasn't sleeping very well, and I suppose that's why,

in the end, she succumbed to a bout of pneumonia.
She simply didn't have any strength left to fight it.'

'I'm sorry.' His eyes had darkened with compassion. 'That must have been terrible for you.'

She closed the dishwasher door and set the controls. 'It was bad.' She was silent for a moment, lost in sad reflection. 'Though what I remember most was feeling bewildered and confused about everything that was happening. They died within a year of each other, and I was left with so many emotions mixed up inside me…hurt, despair, even anger because they had left me alone like that.' She straightened, pulling in a deep breath. 'Of course, the grief lessens with time, but I don't think you can ever really come to terms with losing the people you love.'

'Especially when the end is sudden and unexpected,' he murmured in sympathy, 'and even more so when you're bereaved at a young age. Don't you have any brothers or sisters?'

Mollie shook her head. 'No. My cousin was the nearest I had to a sister.' She thought back over the times she had spent with Laura, the growing-up years, Laura's recent marriage to James, and her expression was bleak for a while.

Then she pulled herself together and went on, 'At the time I felt that I was completely alone in the world, but my uncle and aunt took me in straight away. They were both very kind and supportive and did whatever they could to make me feel that I belonged.'

She made a wry face. 'It can't have been easy for them. I felt so much like a displaced person and, looking back, I'm pretty sure I was awkward and uncooperative to begin with. Added to that they had problems with my cousin because, even though we were friends, she must have resented the sudden intrusion into her life. Who could blame her? She had been their only child, the apple of their eye for so long, and then all at once everything changed when I moved in.'

He frowned. 'This is the Laura whose room I'm using?'

'That's right.'

He fingered the faint stubble along the line of his jaw. 'Is she likely to be coming back and wanting her room in a hurry?'

Her mouth twisted. 'I think you can safely go up and have a shave, and generally make yourself comfortable.' For a moment she hesitated, her mind flicking back over the unexpected pattern events had taken in the past few months, then she added, 'She married several months ago, and has a home of her own now.'

'That's a relief,' he murmured. 'Though I could always have asked for my room back at the pub. The building work at my place may take a week or so yet.'

'There's no need to do that. You're welcome to stay here.' Even though it was unsettling for her to have Sam around, she didn't think the pub was a good idea. It wouldn't have been very comfortable for him to have had to stay in one room for any length of time.

He nodded. 'Thanks. You and your uncle have been very hospitable, putting me up.' He viewed her thoughtfully, 'What happened to your aunt? I haven't heard any mention of her.'

'Aunt Becky died a few years ago.' She didn't want to dwell on that painful time. It still seemed very close to home, and she felt the loss like a heavy ache round her heart. She cleared the huskiness from her throat, and made an effort to go on. 'We became very protective of my uncle after that. The positions were reversed, so to speak—we needed to take care of him—and just lately we've been even more concerned about his welfare.'

'I can understand how you feel.' He moved away from the table, studying her closely, his eyes narrowing as he watched the emotions flicker across her face. 'I heard you mention some tests to him. Did you have anything specific in mind?'

She wondered if he had changed the subject to spare her. She took a deep breath and said, 'I'm just trying to eliminate various possibilities. Pernicious anaemia might account for some of his symptoms, and I think he may be becoming dehydrated so I'd like to check out sodium levels in a urine test. It may come to nothing, but it's worth a try. In the meantime, all I can do is make sure he has every opportunity to get his strength back and keep him from worrying about the practice.'

'Which is where I come in. He'll be easier in his mind, knowing that everything isn't falling on your shoulders.'

'Maybe,' she said guardedly. 'But you know that this could be just a temporary arrangement, don't you? I know he's feeling anxious at the moment, but I can't see him wanting to take a back seat once he's well again. He's always loved being in medicine, and he cares a great deal for his patients. No matter what he says now, he may decide he wants to go on working.'

'And you'd like that.' Sam viewed her curiously. 'Why are you so set against my being here?'

She made a grimace. 'I'm sorry if it appears that way to you. It's just that I'm used to working with my uncle. We get along well, and our views are similar. Whereas you and I—' She broke off, searching for the right words.

'What I mean to say is, we are two very different people, and our attitudes are bound to clash. You've just spent several years working in the city, and you're familiar with a certain way of doing things, but this is very different to what you've been used to. We're a small country practice. The pace is slower, and I can't see you being comfortable with that.

'You strike me as a man who likes things done his own way. You'll want to make changes, to put your stamp on the practice, whereas I'm happy with things the way they are. Things were running very smoothly here with just the two of us when Uncle Robert was well.'

His eyes were dark with scepticism. 'What you mean is you're in a rut.'

His tone mocked her, and her emerald eyes flashed a glittering response. 'Then it's a rut I'm happy in,' she countered fiercely. 'I like the way things are. I like the people and the way that I can get to know everyone properly and watch their children growing up. It's far removed from how a city practice works and it means a lot to me to be part of it. You, on the other hand, spent your childhood here, and yet you couldn't wait to get away. Why else would you choose to go and work in the city?'

He shrugged. 'To see how the other half live… To explore the boundaries and beyond. Is that so strange?' His voice was tinged with cynicism as though he doubted she could understand. 'You want to try it some time. It might loosen some of your preconceived ideas.'

'I'm perfectly at ease with the way I live my life,' she responded stiffly. 'You, though, must have de-cided that things weren't quite what you wanted, and you needed to make a change in yours. That's why you came back here.'

She moved away from the dishwasher before he could reply. 'You'll have to excuse me now, but I have to see to some things. Time's getting on, and after yesterday I'm way behind with everything. Feel free to make yourself comfortable. If you need any-thing, just ask.'

'Thanks,' he said calmly. 'Actually, I want to fam-iliarise myself with some of the software your uncle has installed on the computers at the surgery. He told me the computer in the study here was set up much the same as those so, if it's all right with you, I'll spend some time in there after I've freshened up a bit.'

'Of course. Help yourself.' At least if he was oc-cupied he would be less of a thorn in her side.

'When you're ready,' he murmured as she was turning away. 'I'll give you a hand, if you like, with your uncle's blood test. You'll probably find your fingers are a bit stiff for the next few days.'

His words made her turn back to him. Despite her cautious manner, he was being kind to her, and she said quietly, 'Thank you. It would be awkward for me to do it on my own. Perhaps we could do it later this afternoon.'

He nodded, and made his way to the study.

Mollie looked down at the dressing on her hand and pulled a face. It made sense to take him up on the offer, much as she would rather have done without his help. Just having him near seemed to send her hormones into chaos. She wasn't used to feeling so confused and out of synch with everything.

The rest of the day passed relatively quietly. When she had finished her chores she persuaded Robert to let them take blood samples and urine for testing, and she saw to it that they could be sent off to the laboratory the next day.

After that she spent the afternoon going through some of the files she had brought back with her from the surgery, trying to put them in some kind of order once more. It was a tedious job, and eventually she put them to one side and went to find her uncle and coax him into playing Scrabble with her. Sam joined them at Robert's invitation, and she found her wits sharply tested over the next hour.

It was a welcome break from the worries of the surgery, but it didn't last for long. The phone rang early in the evening, and she answered the call, noting down the details on a pad.

'That was Mrs Fernley,' she told Robert a minute or two later. 'I couldn't make out a lot of what she was saying. She sounded wheezy and a bit distracted, as though she wasn't quite with it. I'd better go and pay her a visit.'

'I'll do it,' Sam cut in. 'This is your day off, re-member?'

'I'll go,' Mollie said firmly. 'Mrs Fernley is an old lady, in her seventies, and she doesn't adjust well to change. You'll probably come as far too great a shock to her, I should imagine, and then she'll have palpitations along with everything else.'

Sam grinned. 'We'll both go, then, and you can introduce me. Driving's going to be awkward for you for the next day or so, with the stitches in your hand, and you'll need me to help out.'

Mollie winced. She had forgotten about that. It looked as though she was going to be needing him for a while at least.

He held open the car door for her, and she slid into the passenger seat, hauling her medical bag onto her lap. It took up a fair amount of room, and she reflected that it would probably be a much better idea to lay it down on the back seat. She wasn't used to sharing a car. Twisting around to lift it over, she leaned towards the driver's side and found herself in a soft collision with Sam, who was reaching out to take the bag from her. His hand brushed the rounded swell of her breast, and she caught her breath in a stunned reaction. Blood pounded through her veins like a hot tidal wave, and her ears started to buzz. Sam froze, and the air around them crackled with tension.

He recovered before she did. 'Sorry,' he muttered thickly, shifting away from her. 'Let me take that for you.' He took the bag from her suddenly boneless fingers and placed it on the back seat, then settled back into his seat and abruptly started the engine.

Mollie was glad he didn't say any more, or expect her to talk. Her mouth and throat had gone as dry as a desert and she didn't think she could have managed a word. She wasn't used to her body going haywire like that, and it bothered her that her senses could fizz out of control like an explosion of fireworks. Perhaps it was all the strain she had been under lately. The hours she had worked had been long and tiring after all. She had tried to deny it, but maybe she did need a helping hand for the next week or so, just until Uncle Robert was feeling better.

They reached Mrs Fernley's house a few minutes later, and by that time Mollie was thankfully feeling more composed. She rang the doorbell and waited while the old lady made her way slowly along the hall. They heard her shuffling footsteps and then the door was opened a crack.

'Who's this?' Mrs Fernley demanded sharply, viewing Sam with deep suspicion. 'I'm not going into a home,' she said wheezily, struggling with the words. 'You're not taking me away. I'm staying here.' She started to push the door closed, and Mollie quickly intervened.

'It's all right, Edie. No one's going to send you away. This is my colleague, Dr Bradley. He's going to be working at the surgery with me while Dr Sinclair is unwell.'

'Is that right?' Edie's breath came in short bursts. 'Well...I suppose you'd better come in, then.' She reluctantly opened the door and let them into the hall. 'Come through to the living-room.'

She led the way into a small back room that looked out onto the garden, a small patch of lawn with raised flower beds to one side and a rockery alongside a stone wall.

'Tell me what's been the matter, Edie,' Mollie said, when they were seated on the chintz-covered sofa. 'Are you having trouble with your breathing?'

'Can't get my breath hardly at all these days. Stops me sleeping.'

Mollie nodded and scooped her stethoscope out of her bag. 'I'd better have a listen to your chest and see if we can find out what's going on in there.'

'Not with t'other one around.' Edie jerked her head in Sam's direction, and Mollie sent him a wry smile. Obligingly, he stepped into the kitchen, and Mollie heard him filling the kettle.

'There's quite a bit of congestion in your chest,' she told the old lady after a while. 'I can hear lots of crackles and wheezes in there. What about your throat—is that sore? Your voice sounds huskier than usual.'

'Just the breathing, that's all. Can't do what I used to. All too much for me lately.'

'That's probably because your body's fighting off a chest infection. I'll give you some antibiotics to clear it up, and you need to rest and drink plenty of fluids in the meantime. You can take paracetamol if you're in any pain.'

Edie buttoned up her blouse and nodded. 'Rest. That's right. But it's noisy round here with the kids.

Rattle the dustbins and tip the milk bottles over. Never used to be like that.'

Mollie made a mental note to have a word with the local constable. Perhaps he could keep an eye on things, move the children on.

Sam came in with a loaded tray and set it down on the table. 'This will make you feel better,' he said. 'Dr Mollie's tablets might clear things up, but you can't beat a cup of tea to put some cheer into you.'

'Drop of whisky in it would do a sight better.'

Sam laughed, a deep rumble in the back of his throat. 'You're right, that would definitely put some colour in your cheeks and a sparkle in your blue eyes. The men at the Evergreen Club had better watch out.'

'Those old devils?' Edie croaked. 'They should be so lucky.'

The two of them exchanged banter for a few minutes longer and then, when their tea was finished, Sam and Mollie went back to the car, leaving the old lady chuckling to herself.

'Do you flirt like that with all your women patients?' Mollie queried with a faintly amused lift of her brow when they were on the road for home. She could see he was going to play havoc with all the females who came to the surgery.

He shook his head. 'Not all of them. Only the pretty ones.'

She made a strangled sound in the back of her throat, and he laughed. 'There's nothing wrong with a light-hearted bit of flirting every now and again. Haven't you ever tried it?' He gave her a speculative look. 'Isn't there a man in your life?'

'That's classified,' she told him.

He gave a wry smile. 'You're leaving me to guess. Intriguing, but at least it wasn't a yes, which means…' He left the statement open, his eyes sparkling with mischief. She recognised that look.

'Forget it,' she said flatly, and she meant it. No man was going to be allowed to creep into her life again. She'd been down that road before, and things hadn't worked out, and she didn't feel like putting herself through that kind of heartache again. Sam was clearly showing an interest in her, but he had to be avoided most of all because there was a definite air of danger about him, a feeling she couldn't explain, but all her instincts told her that she should steer clear of him.

Things were all right the way they were now, neat and tidy, with herself in complete control. That way, nothing could get out of hand. 'I'm not in the market for a relationship,' she said huskily.

'Aren't you?' he murmured, and there was a teasing tilt to his mouth that put her on edge all over again. 'Shame, that. I quite like the idea of getting to know you better.'

He was laughing at her again, and her fingers bunched convulsively in her lap. Why wouldn't he take her seriously? How on earth was she going to get through these next few weeks working alongside this man? He was impossible.

CHAPTER FOUR

GOING back to the surgery on Monday morning was much more of an ordeal than Mollie had expected. She had thought she was over the break-in, but her confidence must have been misplaced because she found that her fingers were trembling a little as she opened the door. She looked around the place warily, not altogether sure what she might find waiting for her.

'Are you OK?' Sam asked, a note of concern in his voice, and she brought her attention back to him a little jerkily.

'I'm fine,' she murmured. 'I suppose I half thought the vandals might have been back, but it was just my nerves playing up. It wasn't really very likely that they would come anywhere near the place.'

'It was a nasty experience you went through, but you won't need to worry about it for much longer,' he said firmly. 'I've arranged for a security expert to come along and talk to me about the various options this morning.'

Mollie blinked in surprise. 'When did you sort that out?'

'On Saturday, when we had finished here.'

She pulled in a sharp breath. He was taking charge again, wasn't he? It was only Monday now, his first proper day at the surgery, and already he had been organising things without telling her first. The man was thoroughly exasperating. Give him an inch, and where would it end?

She said pointedly, 'At the weekend, when you said you were going to look into it, I didn't imagine you would go ahead and arrange things without talking to me first. I'd actually planned on looking into it myself today.'

He shrugged. 'I've saved you a job, then. I felt that it was something that needed to be dealt with right away, and you had other things on your mind at the time. After I've heard what the man has to say, we'll set up an alarm system that will make you feel much safer.'

She frowned, thinking back over Saturday's events. Sam had made some phone calls, she remembered, but she'd had no idea that he'd acted so quickly, and the knowledge that he would do it without consulting her first was unsettling. He certainly didn't mean to let the grass grow under his feet, did he?

'I'm glad you said *we*,' she returned stiffly. She needed to know that things weren't going to get out of hand, that she was always fully aware of what was going on, and she wasn't about to let him come in here and walk all over her like that. She opened her mouth to tell him as much, then had to bite back the words as the door opened and the receptionist walked into the room.

Caroline was carrying a tray laden with cups, and she set it down carefully on the counter, before turning towards them, an inquisitive smile on her face. She was a slim young woman, with wavy fair hair and calm grey eyes.

'Hello, there,' she greeted them both. 'I thought you might be ready for this.' The enticing aroma of coffee filled the air, and Mollie sniffed appreciatively. Caroline was a treasure to have around. She could always be relied on to run things smoothly, to be quietly efficient, and Mollie would be lost without her.

Mollie felt obliged to push down her rising feelings of annoyance with Sam and introduce him.

Caroline smiled up at him. 'It'll be good to have you with us,' she said cheerfully. 'Mollie's had such a lot on her plate lately, and she could do with someone to share the load.' Ignoring Mollie's frown, she added, 'She phoned me and told me that you had helped her to clear the place up on Saturday. I can't imagine what it would have been like to come in here today and find everything upside down, and patients waiting to be seen. Has there been any word from the police?'

He shook his head. 'Nothing at all. It might just be one of those things that you have to put behind you and mark down to experience.'

'That's all we can do.' She grimaced. 'Though we're still suffering the aftermath. Goodness knows how long it will take me to put the rest of the files back in order, but I'll make a start right away and try to fit it in between surgeries.'

'Thanks,' Mollie said. 'With a bit of luck they won't be too chaotic.' She shot a glance over the waiting-room, and saw that it was beginning to fill up quite rapidly. 'I'd better go to my room and sort myself out. Give me five minutes, then send the first patient along, will you?' There was no time right then to deal with the problem of Sam and his high-handed ways. She would have to think it through after she had finished work.

'Will do.' Caroline consulted her list. 'It looks as though your first patient is Mrs Ralston. There shouldn't be a problem—her notes will be on your computer. It was only the computers in Reception that were damaged.'

Mollie nodded, and went off to make herself ready for surgery, taking her coffee with her and leaving Sam to study his own schedule for the morning.

Mrs Ralston put her head round her door a minute or two later. She was a woman in her late twenties in a clearly advanced state of pregnancy.

'How are you, Jenny?' Mollie queried. Eyeing the woman's large bump, she added, 'You must be very near to time. When is the baby due?'

Jenny made a wry smile. 'The end of next week, but it feels as though it could be any minute. This last month has been really uncomfortable, and I just wish it would all be over and done with.' She put a hand over her abdomen and sighed. 'I keep telling him he knows the way out and to get a move on, but he's just not listening to me.'

Mollie laughed. 'I'm sure he'll come when he's ready. You're having a hospital birth, aren't you?'

'That's right. There were problems with my first— she wasn't head down and I very nearly had to have a Caesarean, so to be on the safe side I need to go in for this one.'

Mollie nodded. 'I remember. She's a lively little two-year-old now, though, from what I've seen.' She smiled, and waved a hand towards the couch. 'If you'll go and lie down I'll check you over.'

Jenny did as she was asked, and Mollie made a brief examination and listened to the baby's heart-beat. 'That sounds fine,' she murmured, 'and the head's definitely engaged so it shouldn't be too long now.'

'Tell him that,' Jenny groaned. 'He's been press-ing on my bladder for the last three weeks and I can't stop running to the toilet.'

Mollie smiled in sympathy, winding the blood-pressure cuff around Jenny's arm. 'After the first child the muscles down there might be a bit more relaxed, and the baby generally feels as though it's lower down.' She checked the blood-pressure gauge. 'That's higher than normal, but nothing to worry about. OK, you can get dressed now. Are you man-aging to rest at all in the daytime?'

Jenny's brows shot up. 'With Amy running me ragged? You must be joking. I can't move from one room to another without feeling as though I'm under siege. It doesn't help with Alan working away in Whitby either.'

'It must be difficult for you.' Mollie glanced through the notes on screen while Jenny dressed. 'Your urine sample was OK, no sugar in it, and your blood test shows that your iron level has risen. Have you been taking iron tablets?'

Jenny shook her head. 'Cereals, every morning, that's what's done it. I feel fitter for having breakfast. I don't always feel like eating first thing, but I de-cided I needed the energy.'

'Well, it certainly seems to have done the trick.

Keep up the good work, and try to find time to put your feet up, even if it means putting a video on for Amy to watch.'

'That's a good idea. I might just try it this afternoon.' Jenny was looking thoughtful as she left the room.

Mollie made steady progress through her list, but it was almost lunchtime when her last patient, a woman in her late forties, came in.

'Hello, Mrs Carter. What can I do for you?'

'I've come about a pain I've had for the last few days.' Mrs Carter chewed at her lip. 'It started here.' She put a hand to her back at waist level on her right side. 'Then, the day before yesterday, in the night, I woke up with waves of pain all across here.' This time, she ran her hand over the region around her navel. 'And in the morning the pain was in both the back and the front on this side. It felt really nasty, and now, today, my skin around here is really sore.' She made a half-circle to show the area around her right hip from back to front. 'Just the feel of my dress on my skin makes it really hurt.'

'I think I'd better take a look,' Mollie said. 'Let me see your skin, where it's sore, to begin with.'

Mrs Carter showed her, but said in a bewildered tone, 'There's nothing there. I already looked.'

Mollie nodded, agreeing that the skin was unblemished. 'But you say it's sore to the touch round here?'

'Yes. It feels like bad sunburn.'

'OK.' Mollie went over to the couch. 'Hop up on here and I'll examine you.'

After a few minutes, when she had completed the examination and Mrs Carter was getting dressed, she said, 'You do seem to be suffering some general abdominal discomfort, but your symptoms could indicate one or two different things. I notice from your records that you have had some ulceration at some time in your stomach and the intestine, and it's possible that there might be some inflammation arising from that. You can take an antacid to relieve it. On the other hand, the soreness of the skin that you're describing sounds very much as though you might be about to develop shingles.'

Mrs Carter winced. 'Oh, dear. I've heard about that. Isn't it something to do with the chickenpox virus?'

'That's right. If you get chickenpox as a child, some of the virus can lie dormant in the body for many years. Then, in some people, when the body's defences are low the virus can re-emerge and cause shingles.' She paused and studied the woman thoughtfully. 'You've not been in the best of health lately, have you?'

'I've been feeling under the weather for most of the year, really,' the woman acknowledged ruefully. 'It's been one thing after another. Colds, chest infections, sore throats. I just haven't been able to get on top of any of it.'

Mollie nodded. 'It sounds as though you're generally run-down, and therefore you might be more liable to attack by the shingles virus. The area you've shown me is a prime site for it, so if you do start to get a rash in the next few days you should come and see me straight away. If treatment is started as soon as the rash appears, it can help prevent long-term problems.'

Mrs Carter looked anxious. 'What kind of problems do you mean?'

'The shingles virus attacks a nerve in the body,
and it can cause damage to that nerve, which might
result in long-term pain for months or possibly years
after the rash has subsided. The good news, though,
is that if you come to the surgery as soon as the rash
appears, I can give you a course of treatment that
should minimise that long-term damage. If you delay
in coming to me once the rash appears then it will
be too late and the treatment won't work.'

Mrs Carter drew in a deep breath. 'If anything de-
velops, I'll make sure I come back.' She smiled.
'Thank you for explaining things to me, Doctor.'

'You're welcome.'

After Mrs Carter had gone, Mollie went back to
Reception and sifted through the post that Caroline
had put in her tray. Sam appeared as she was signing
forms, and she looked up and asked, 'How did your
morning go?'

'Well enough, on the whole,' he said, pulling a
wry face, 'but the patients are a bit dubious about
me, I think.'

She grinned. 'They'll get used to you, given time.
We're a bit of a close community around here.'

'So I gather.' He tossed a bundle of patients' notes
into his tray. 'Have you made any plans for lunch?
Since we're sharing transport, we ought to liaise as
much as we can.'

'I wanted to go home and check up on Uncle
Robert,' she said, grimacing, 'but there are a number
of home visits to do, as well as the late afternoon
appointments to fit in. As things are, I'm going to

have to grab a quick sandwich from the local bakery and start on the calls fairly soon. Luckily, there's nothing that sounds too urgent.'

'OK. I'll go and get some lunch with you, and on the way I can fill you in on the details of my meeting with the security man. We'll do the visits just as soon as you're ready. I'm sure your uncle knows how things are, and he can always reach you on the mobile if he's in trouble.'

Mollie nodded. 'I know that,' she said, reaching for her jacket and slipping it on over her cool linen dress. 'It's just that I worry about him.'

They walked the short distance to the bakery, and on the way Sam told her about the suggested plan to make the surgery more secure, with video cameras and special lighting that would be triggered whenever someone approached the building. She didn't like the thought of having to take such precautions in what had always been a small and friendly practice, but despite her reservations she couldn't see an alternative. The whole incident had shaken her up, and she needed to feel that something was being done to prevent a repeat of it.

Sam explained that there would also be individual panic alarms, and she had to admit that those would make her feel a lot safer.

'It will probably cost a fortune,' she commented wryly. 'I'm not sure the practice can afford it.'

'We'll work something out,' he said easily as they reached the shop. 'We'll go over the accounts and see if there's anywhere we can make cuts. I expect some changes can be made to make things more efficient.'

She reflected on that briefly. 'Some *minor* changes,' she said sternly.

He gave a crooked grin. 'We have to do something, anyway. The insurance company will probably insist on it after what happened.'

He was probably right about that, Mollie reflected as she scanned the bakery shelves and picked out a salad sandwich and a bun. Sam made his selection, and they went outside to eat, sitting on a bench on the green, overlooking a small stream. In front of them a small group of children played noisily on the grass while their mothers chatted.

Beside her on the bench, Sam shifted lazily and stretched out his long legs, the fabric of his trousers straining tautly over the hard muscles of his thighs as he moved. Watching him, Mollie felt a warm, unexpected quiver of awareness ripple through her, and quickly turned her gaze away.

'This place is still as beautiful as I remembered,' Sam murmured. 'I came back expecting to find it changed, but it hasn't, it's totally unspoiled. There are still the same quaint old shops, the little paved squares and open spaces.'

'Didn't you go away because you were bored with all that?'

His mouth curved wryly. 'Not at all. I wanted to learn more about the way things work in the city, I wanted to know at firsthand how the cogs of the big machine worked, and I wanted to be part of it.'

'And now?'

'Now I can see the wider picture, and I realise I can't reconcile myself to the impersonal nature of medicine in the big institutions. I can't go along with the idea that patients are simply customers availing themselves of a service. It seems altogether too cold a way of thinking for me. Like you said yourself, it's people who matter, and having time to get to know them and treat them throughout their lives is part of the caring process that makes the job satisfying.'

'So you didn't enjoy your time in the city?'

'I wouldn't say that necessarily. It was good experience and I met some dedicated people, but most of all it gave me a better perspective on things.'

Out of the blue, just then a child's multi-coloured plastic ball came flying towards them. Sam caught it deftly with one hand and then twirled it lightly in his fingers.

'Sorry, mister.' A small boy walked up to them, his eyes wide, his lips parted in expectation, and with a smile Sam gently tossed the ball back.

'Fanks.' The child ran away to join his friends, and Mollie watched them start their game all over again, smiling at their shouts of childish laughter.

Sam glanced down at his watch. 'Lovely as it is out here,' he murmured, 'I think we ought to be making a move.'

She nodded, stretching her limbs to ease the muscles, and began to gather her things together. 'Young Lee Simmons is first on the list, isn't he? I want to see if there's any improvement after his asthma attack at the weekend.'

Some ten minutes later they arrived at Lee's house, and Sam and the boy clapped their palms together in a typically male salute. Lee's cheeky grin told Mollie that he was definitely on the mend, which was an enormous relief, even though he still looked pale and she couldn't help noticing that there wasn't much flesh on his thin little frame.

'He's been OK,' his mother told them, ruffling his hair affectionately. 'A lot quieter than usual, though, considering how lively he is normally.' Her eyes suddenly shimmered, and she blinked quickly. 'I never thought the day would come when I'd actually want him to be jumping around, getting into mischief,' she said in a choked voice.

Mollie put a reassuring hand on her arm. 'He looks bright enough in himself today. Children are very resilient, you know. After he's had a day or so's rest, I'm sure you'll be happily tearing your hair out again.'

Mrs Simmons laughed weakly. 'I hope so.'

Sam was delving into his medical bag, and Lee asked curiously, 'Are you goin' to use that listening thing again?'

Sam nodded. 'I think it might be a good idea to listen to your chest again to see if your lungs are a bit clearer. Do you want to have a listen as well?'

Lee nodded excitedly, and Sam grinned and gave him the earpieces of the stethoscope, placing the diaphragm on his chest. Absorbed, the child listened to the noises from his lungs. He laughed. 'Crackle, squidge.'

'Yes, you're right,' Sam told him after he had examined him. 'There are a few crackles in there still, but you're definitely sounding better than you did before. I think we'll do a peak flow reading. Can you blow into the meter for me?'

Lee obliged, and inspected the meter along with Sam, his nose wrinkling in a frown. 'Is that good?'

'It is—much better than last time. Are you using your inhaler as I showed you?'

Lee nodded vigorously.

'Good. Let me see you use it now.' Sam watched the boy closely as he inhaled the bronchodilator drug, and then tweaked his shoulder gently in satisfaction.

'Well done.' He turned to Mrs Simmons. 'I think we can safely say that he's on the mend now. We'll try to build him up with a food supplement and extra vitamins, and when next you come into the asthma clinic we'll see how he's progressing. In the meantime, give us a ring if ever you need anything.'

'I will. Thanks.'

They left the house to go on with the visits, and Mollie commented quietly, 'You were very good with him. You have a flair for dealing with children.'

Sam's brows lifted in surprise. 'I hadn't thought about it. I suppose I'm used to being around my nephews and nieces. They're round about Lee's age, or younger, full of life and expectation.'

They finished the rest of the visits, taking it in turn to deal with each patient. Mollie hadn't wanted the enforced company on her rounds, but she had to admit it gave her a good opportunity to introduce Sam to the patients, and she was able to watch him in action. He was gentle, compassionate and undeniably caring, and he seemed to have an unerring instinct for the right way to handle each patient. She was impressed in spite of herself.

They returned to the surgery for the late afternoon appointments, and she wondered if half the people that turned up were there out of curiosity, wanting to see the new doctor. As it was, it was some two hours later that Sam saw the last patient out of his room.

Mollie put her head round his door, and he smiled ruefully. 'Ready to go home?' he asked, and she nodded. It had been a long day.

The journey back to the house shouldn't take them more than ten minutes or so, and Mollie was looking forward to a soak in the bath and the supper of hot chicken casserole which she had prepared that morning.

Her anticipation was short-lived, though, because some halfway along the route on the main road they were flagged down by an agitated-looking woman who was standing beside her car at the side of the road.

Sam pulled up alongside and stuck his head out of the window. 'Something wrong? Can we help at all?'

'My friend's in the car,' the woman said in a rush, pushing her hand distractedly through her thick, dark hair. 'The ambulance didn't turn up—I didn't know what to do, so I started out for the hospital.'

Sam was out of the car in a flash, and Mollie followed swiftly, grabbing her medical bag. She recognised the woman as one of her weight-watcher patients.

'Try to keep calm, Anna, and tell us what the problem is.'

'Oh—Dr Mollie, it's you. Thank heaven.' Anna flapped a hand in the direction of her car. 'It's Jenny. She's having her baby, and I think something's wrong. It all started happening so suddenly, the midwife was out on another call, and we just daren't wait for the ambulance any longer—she's been feeling the urge to push for ages.'

Mollie hurried towards the car and saw that Jenny Ralston was in the back seat, obviously distressed and in pain, with small beads of sweat breaking out on her brow. Sam was already on the phone, stabbing in the numbers for back-up.

'How often are the contractions coming, Jenny?' Mollie asked, making a hurried examination. The membranes had ruptured, and it appeared that she was fully dilated, but there wasn't room for the head to emerge without risking a tear to the mother's tissues.

'Every minute or so,' Jenny gasped. 'It hurts so much. Can you do something?'

'We'll look after you, Jenny,' she murmured quietly, and quickly introduced Sam, though she suspected Jenny was too preoccupied to care very much who was there. 'Don't worry. Just concentrate on your breathing with each contraction.'

She pulled out a foetal stethoscope from her bag and put it to Jenny's abdomen. There were clear signs of foetal distress, with a slower than normal heartbeat, and Mollie was worried about the risks to the baby if he wasn't delivered quickly.

'She's going to need an episiotomy,' she told Sam. She looked down at her bandaged hand and bit her lip. Her injuries hadn't healed yet, and she wasn't sure she could handle the instruments adequately to make the necessary cut. It was upsetting, not being able to look after Jenny properly, and she said unhappily, 'I don't know if—'

'I'll do it,' Sam said. 'You concentrate on moni-
toring the baby.'

'OK. If you're sure?' There wasn't time for delay,
and she struggled to overcome the bitter frustration
she felt at being unable to take charge of the situation.

'I am.' He worked fast, injecting the site and then,
when the anaesthetic had taken effect, made a neat
cut. 'Another contraction, Jenny. Push. I can see the
baby's head. That's it, push again.' The process was
repeated with the next few contractions, but the baby
wasn't moving and Jenny was quickly becoming
tired. 'Push, Jenny,' Sam said again.

'I'm trying. Really, I'm trying.' Jenny's voice rose
in a wail of misery. 'It's not happening, is it?' Her
voice broke and she began to cry, aching sobs that
racked her body, and Mollie stroked her face with a
gentle, soothing motion.

'You're doing very well,' she murmured. 'Take
your time and rest till the next contraction. Relax,
now.' Even though she spoke the reassuring words,
Mollie was feeling increasingly worried. With each
contraction of the womb, the baby's oxygen supply
was being depleted.

Her glance shot across to Sam. 'We need a ventouse,' she muttered.

He nodded. 'You're right. There's one in the boot
of my car... There should be a blanket in there as
well,' he added on an afterthought.

She pulled in a quick breath. 'I'll get them.'

She carefully eased herself away from Jenny, and
ran over to the car, grabbing everything she needed
from the boot and hurrying back. Anna had taken

over the role of supporting her friend, and Mollie turned her attention to the baby's struggling heartbeat once more.

She handed Sam the suction cup of the ventouse just as another contraction began, and he applied the cup to the baby's head, gently pulling on the traction bar to try to ease the baby's head out of the birth canal. It was a slow process, and Mollie found herself saying a silent prayer.

Then, all at once, it was over. The head was out, followed by one shoulder, then the other, and finally the baby emerged completely. Sam carefully moved the cord from around the baby's neck, and tipped the infant head down to draw the mucus from its air passages.

Mollie found she was holding her breath, but in the next moment there was a soft little cry, a tiny protest at the indignity of birth, and her eyes filled with a sheen of tears, her throat aching with joy and wonder.

'It's a boy, Jenny,' she whispered. The infant cried again, louder this time, and Mollie choked on a muffled laugh. 'A very cross little boy.'

Jenny put her arms out for the child and they laid him carefully on her belly. Sam clamped the cord and cut it, and gave the mother an injection to help expel the placenta, while Mollie tenderly placed the blanket around mother and son. A minute or two later they heard the ambulance siren.

They stood together and watched the ambulance pull away with its precious cargo a few minutes later, and waved Anna off in her car. Mollie struggled with a lump in her throat, and tried to blink away the tears she felt stinging her eyelids. She felt Sam's concerned gaze move over her, and didn't want him to know how oddly feminine and vulnerable she felt right then.

'You're not worried about them, are you?' he asked softly. She shook her head, not able to trust her voice to answer him. 'They'll be fine,' he murmured. 'The baby's in an incubator, and he'll be given oxygen and be kept under observation, but I don't believe he's come to any real harm. Any longer, out on the highway without help, perhaps, and he might have been in real trouble, but we were there and we managed to bring him into the world in time.'

'You were there,' she managed huskily. 'You did it. I was useless. I couldn't do anything.' She pressed her lips together and swallowed hard to keep back the tears that threatened to overwhelm her.

'Hey,' Sam murmured gently, 'what's all this?' His arms went around her and he drew her to him, pulling her into the warm shelter of his body. 'You were marvellous. You were calm and collected, you knew exactly what had to be done. How can you say you were useless?'

Miserably, she flung her bandaged hand aimlessly into the air. 'If you hadn't been there, if it had been left to me, the baby might have died...' She began to cry softly. 'Or suffered brain damage...or—'

'Or nothing,' he cut in, giving her a little shake. 'You're overwrought and not thinking straight. You'd have managed just fine if I hadn't been there. Maybe a little clumsy because of your damaged hand but, believe me, you'd have coped very well, even without a ventouse, because your fingers are much smaller and more dextrous than mine. At the very worst you would have been able to tell Anna what to do. You're being too hard on yourself.'

She shook her head, burying her face in his shirt front, and he held onto her, soothing her with soft words, his hands lightly stroking along her spine.

'It's all right,' he murmured. 'Believe me. You've nothing to blame yourself for.'

'He was such a lovely baby, so beautiful. I couldn't have borne it if—'

'Stop thinking that way.' He looked down at her upturned face, her cheeks damp with tears, and he reached up to cup her face and kiss her gently on the mouth, successfully quieting the words that hovered there.

Whatever she had been about to say went completely out of her head. Mollie felt the brush of his lips on hers and a shaft of intense heat lanced through her, striking at the very core of her being. Her world started to spiral out of control and she clung to him dizzily, her fingers closing on the bunched muscles of his arms. Her knees went weak, and her body, suddenly soft and supple, melted against the hard strength of his.

He groaned, a deep, rumbling sound in his throat, his hands moving over her body with tender, possessive caresses. Her breath snagged in her throat as she, in turn, tentatively explored the wide sweep of his shoulders, her fingertips sliding over the firm contours of his back. She was light-headed, trembling with a stunning awakening of desire which had caught her unawares.

'Ah, Mollie,' he whispered, his mouth teasing her lips, spreading fire through every fibre of her being. 'You feel good, so good. So sweetly feminine. I didn't realise how long I've been aching to kiss you.'

His hands slid smoothly over the rounded contours of her body, arching her against his heated thighs, and she gave a shuddery gasp, swaying a little as his palm moved up to caress the full, soft curve of her breast. Her bones were melting, her body was consumed by flame. It would be so easy to let herself give in to the tide of passion that was flowing through her veins, to forget everything for just a moment in time.

But she knew that it couldn't last, didn't she? That it was only a momentary thing, this feeling of desperate need, a fleeting sensation of happiness that would melt away like a snowflake in the first rays of the sun. She hardly knew Sam, and even if she was tempted to give herself up to the sweet sensations that surged through her while she was in his arms it would more than likely end in tears. She had been hurt before, and she didn't want to put herself through that again.

The heat haze slowly evaporated from her mind, and her thoughts gradually reassembled themselves into something more sane and realistic. She tried to ease herself away from him, pressing the flat of her hands against his chest when he would have resisted.

'I can't,' she whispered. 'I can't do this.'

'Why not?' His head was bent towards her, his lips still only fractionally away from hers. 'You were with me just then, you wanted me. You returned my kisses. You don't mean what you're saying, do you?'

'I do,' she said huskily, her breathing ragged. 'I'm sorry. I should never have let it happen. I'm not ready for this.'

She heard the swift intake of his breath. 'Why, Mollie? I don't understand.' He frowned suddenly, a nerve pulsing in his jaw. 'Is there someone else?'

She shook her head, the shimmer of tears bright in her eyes.

He studied her, his eyes dark, flickering with doubt. 'But there was someone... Is that it?'

'Yes,' she whispered, 'there was someone. But it's over now, it's in the past, and I don't want to talk about it.' She pulled away from him.

'Mollie, you can't just leave it like that.' His voice was threaded through with exasperation.

She sucked in a deep breath. 'That's how I want it,' she said flatly. 'Buried, and forgotten, and not to be resurrected.'

'That won't work, you must know that deep down.' His voice was rough edged, his expression taut. 'Sometimes things need to be brought out into the open and faced squarely. Running away is no solution.'

'I'm managing just fine.'

'Are you?' His mouth tightened. 'It seems to me that you're taking the coward's way out.'

His words stung, and it bothered her that he must despise her for her weakness, but she didn't answer. Then she heard the sound of a car engine thrumming in the distance, and she turned to watch its progress.

'Will you take me home?' she asked. 'I'm really very tired.'

CHAPTER FIVE

AN UNEXPECTED visitor was waiting for them when they arrived back at the house. Conscious of the strained atmosphere between herself and Sam, Mollie was almost glad of the diversion.

Laura was in the kitchen, sitting at the table, leafing her way through a magazine, but she rose fluidly to her feet when they came in, slender and attractive, and as vivacious as ever, and greeted them with a warm smile.

'Hi, Mollie.' Laura came towards her with her arms outstretched and gave her a big hug, and Mollie found herself enveloped in a sweet-smelling cloud of perfume. Her cousin's glossy raven hair flicked in a silky swathe across her cheek.

'It seems like ages since I've seen you,' Mollie commented lightly. 'Well, it must be three or four weeks at least.'

'You've been out the last few times I've dropped by. You're obviously very busy these days.' There was a momentary hint of seriousness in Laura's expression, but it quickly vaporised and she straightened up, saying, 'But at least you've some help at the surgery now, from what I've been hearing.'

She turned to Sam. 'Is this the new doctor? Sam, is that right?' She held out her hand to him. 'I'm Laura.' Her blue eyes, as clear and bright as corn-

flowers, swept over him, registering approval. 'My
dad's been telling me all about you.'

'Good things, I hope?' Sam returned the smile,
interest sparking in his eyes as he took Laura's hand
firmly in his.

'Definitely. It'll make a lot of difference, having
you around, I'm sure. Perhaps he'll be able to rest
more easily now, knowing that everything isn't falling on Mollie's shoulders.'

'That's the general idea.'

'How are you settling in? Have Mollie and my dad
made you feel at home?'

Mollie watched the two of them and felt oddly like
an outsider. It was a feeling she ought to be used to
where Laura was concerned, she acknowledged ruefully. Hadn't it always been like that? Laura had such
a lively, magnetic personality that she drew everyone
to her, particularly the opposite sex, and Mollie was
frequently left with a distant kind of feeling, as
though she didn't quite belong.

It wasn't Laura's fault. She was beautiful and un-
selfconsciously at ease with the people around her,
and the frequent result was that men couldn't help
falling under her spell.

Mollie, on the other hand, was well aware that she
was more reserved, made cautious, perhaps, by the
way her parents had been taken from her at an early
age. It was a fault, she couldn't deny it, but it was
beyond her to know how to behave any differently.
It wasn't easy to be open-hearted and free with your
feelings when you knew that happiness could be
whipped out from under your feet at any time.

That's why her relationship with James had been

so special. He had seemed to understand her shyness, her need to take her time in getting to know him properly. He had been kind and considerate, a true friend—or so she had thought until he, too, had met Laura and had fallen for her winning ways.

She didn't resent Laura for that. It was just the way things were, but even so Mollie struggled to suppress the familiar pangs of loneliness and isolation that sometimes welled up and made her heart feel like a lead weight. She was right to avoid any kind of involvement, wasn't she? In the end it was always too painful.

'How is he, Mollie?'

'Sorry?' Laura's words brought her back to the present with a jolt, and she collected herself, faint colour creeping along her cheek-bones.

'You were miles away,' Laura said, unperturbed. 'I was asking how Dad is, whether you're any nearer to finding out what's causing his problems? There's not much point in me asking Dad because he just fobs me off and tries to make out everything's OK when I can see perfectly well that it's not. At least I managed to persuade him to go and lie down for a while, though.'

On safer ground, Mollie cleared her throat. 'We're still waiting for test results. All I can do in the meantime is to keep an eye on him, although that's difficult with me being out most of the day. I do worry about him.'

Laura's gaze was thoughtful. 'Perhaps I can help out a bit, at least over this next fortnight. I'm due some time off from work so I could look in on him

every day, perhaps keep him company in the after-
noons until you get back.'

'What work do you do?' Sam asked.

'I'm a rep for a pharmaceutical company. Generally I tend to do a lot of travelling about, but they're
reorganising just now and it's a convenient time for
me to take a break. I haven't had any time off since
my wedding so I'm due for some leave.'

'It'll certainly be a relief to know that you'll be
here to watch over him,' Mollie said. 'He's been getting worse of late, more tired and much weaker generally, though I try to make sure he eats regularly
and that he gets out into the fresh air whenever possible. He used to love the garden, but he doesn't
seem to be very interested nowadays. His friends call
in on him, but he's very low-spirited at times.'

Laura nodded, and said thoughtfully, 'Maybe a
change of scene will cheer him up. I'm having a
barbecue on Friday evening, so if we can persuade
him to come along that might help. He won't have
to do anything except relax. We've had such lovely
weather lately, and it will be fun to sit outside and
make the most of it. Besides, we never got around
to a house-warming party, so maybe this will serve
instead. You will come, won't you, Mollie? And you,
Sam.' She smiled up at Sam, and it was as though
the sun had come out in its full glory. 'You must
come, too.'

'I'll look forward to it,' he murmured.

'Good. Right, then, that's settled. I must be off, or
James will be wondering what's happened to me.'

Mollie saw her to the door, and waved her off a
little abstractedly. Laura hadn't waited for her reply

to the invitation, assuming that she would go along as a matter of course, but she didn't much relish the idea of visiting Laura and James in their new home. She frowned. It would be difficult, meeting up with James again. So far she had managed to avoid him on the occasions when he and Laura had visited as a couple because she had been out on call. This, though, was a situation that would be less easily resolved. Perhaps she could plead pressure of work.

She went back into the kitchen where Sam was looking at the country life calendar hanging on the wall. As he lifted his hands to flick through the pages, Mollie watched the subtle interplay of muscle and sinew across his broad back. She recalled the feel of his strong shoulders beneath her fingers and her limbs trembled in reaction. Had that short interlude out on the road changed everything?

She didn't want to spoil the easy working relationship which had been growing between her and Sam, but she was very much afraid things could not be the same.

He turned to face her, his blue eyes cool and strangely remote, and a cold shiver passed through her.

'They're all scenes from around here,' she told him, in an attempt to break the sudden tension that filled the atmosphere.

'I noticed.' His face was shuttered, he wasn't giving anything away, and she moistened her dry lips with her tongue.

Moving over to the hob, she said lightly, 'I'd better start thinking about making some supper.'

'Not for me. I have to go out.'

He walked out of the room, and a few minutes later she heard the front door close behind him and then the crunch of his car tyres on the gravel drive. She felt a strange emptiness inside.

At the surgery over the next few days there was plenty to keep them occupied, and there were more call-outs than usual, with a viral infection doing the rounds and a crop of children's ailments to be dealt with.

Moving from one crisis to another, there was little opportunity to get together with Sam in anything but a professional way, and his manner was always distant. Mollie wasn't sure how she felt about that. Her emotions were confused, chaotic. Part of her yearned for the easy friendship they'd had before, and she found herself torn between wanting him near yet needing, for her own self-preservation, to keep a safe distance between them.

On Friday, her last patient of the morning was Mrs Carter, who appeared to be in some pain, wincing as she sat down.

'What can I do for you, Mrs Carter?' Mollie asked, giving the woman a quick smile before consulting the notes on her screen.

'You said the other day that I might be developing shingles, and I should come back if I started to get a rash,' Mrs Carter explained. 'Well, I don't know if it constitutes a rash exactly, but I've found seven or eight spots that have either come out properly or are just beginning.'

'I'd better take a look,' Mollie said, getting to her feet.

Mrs Carter showed her the same area as before, in an arc around the right side of her waist and hip, and there were definite signs of a rash developing. Mollie inspected it carefully, then asked Mrs Carter to sit down again.

'Is your skin still sensitive?' she asked.

'Yes, it is, very much so, all around that side. It's like a strong burning sensation, but not only that—it hurts inside as well.'

Mollie nodded. 'I'm afraid I do believe it is shingles,' she murmured, 'so I think we must start you on a course of anti-viral medication straight away. Take one tablet five times a day, at regular intervals, for seven days. You'll probably find that a few more spots will come out over the next day or so, while the medication takes time to get a hold, but after that it should stop the virus from developing any further...and that means we can effectively limit any long-term damage.'

She printed out a prescription and handed it to the woman. 'You can take a painkiller at the same time, if you need one—paracetamol would be fine.'

Mrs Carter accepted the prescription gratefully, and said, 'Will it be all right if I dab calamine lotion on the spots? They're very itchy, as well as being sore.'

'Yes, that will be OK. It should help.'

She saw Mrs Carter out, and made her way to Reception. Sam was already there, sitting at one of the desks signing repeat prescriptions, and he looked up, frowning, as she approached.

'All finished for the morning?' he queried briskly 'You seem to have had a long session today.' H swivelled his chair around so that he was facing her properly, then stretched his legs, easing them out from the cramped confines of the desk.

She tried to ignore the flutter in her stomach at the sight of those long legs. 'All done at last. Perhaps we'll soon be over the worst of this latest spate.'

'Let's hope so.' He got to his feet and scooped up the bundle of prescriptions, then came over to her at the reception desk, his body taut as he reached across her for paper clips. Her heart thumped heavily in response to his nearness, and her mouth went dry as a ripple of physical awareness shot through her. She made an effort to concentrate as he spoke again.

'As soon as you're ready, after lunch, we can make a start on the home visits, and then with luck we might be back in time to make an early start on the afternoon appointments. From the looks of things, there aren't too many so far, and between us we should be able to see them off fairly quickly, barring call-outs.'

She mumbled something in reply, and he sent her a sharp glance, before securing the bundle of signed prescriptions with a clip and placing them in Caroline's tray. 'We might even manage to finish on time and not have to rush to get ready for your cousin's barbecue this evening. What time were you planning on getting there?'

Mollie chewed at her lip. 'I don't think I'll be able to manage this evening,' she said slowly. 'I've really too much to do... But that shouldn't affect you at all. I'm sure Laura will be glad to see you—any time after six, I should imagine. My uncle will be able to show you how to get there.' She picked up a manila folder from the table and took it over to the filing cabinet. Away from him she found she could breathe much more easily.

Sam's dark brows came together. 'You're not serious, are you? Your cousin will be expecting you.'

'Oh, she won't worry if I'm not there,' Mollie returned airily, trying to convince herself. 'She knows what the pressures of this job are like and, anyway, there will be plenty of other people around to keep her busy.' She pulled a wry face. 'There really is a lot of paperwork I must catch up on. It's been piling up over the last few weeks while I was on my own, and I can't put it off any longer.' She flashed the file briefly in front of him, before pulling open a drawer of the cabinet. 'This is just one of them.'

His eyes narrowed on her. 'That's just an excuse,' he said, his mouth moving in a sceptical line. 'You don't have to do your paperwork this very evening. If it's waited this long, it can wait a day or so more.'

Mollie shook her head. 'It can't. There are hospital forms which have to be sent off tomorrow, and funding forms which have to be in by a certain date. I don't see any way round it. Anyway, it really doesn't matter. I'm not a party animal, and I shan't mind at all if I stay at home.' She stuffed the file into the drawer.

'Well, I do mind,' he said grimly. 'It isn't healthy to concentrate on work to the extent that you shut yourself away from family and friends. I'm not going to sit back and watch you behave like a martyr when there's no need for it.' His eyes searched her face with the precision of a laser beam, making her acutely uncomfortable. 'I don't know what you problem is, but I'm not going to let you set up barriers around yourself and try to back out of anything that smells of relaxation.'

Her green eyes flashed with annoyance. 'There's no need for you to get involved at all. This is my decision. It has nothing to do with you. It isn't your problem.'

His mouth tightened. 'I'm making it mine,' he said forcefully. 'One way or another, you need to spend some time away from the house and the surgery. For far too long now you've been putting everything you've got into work, and leaving nothing for yourself. That has to stop or you could find yourself sliding rapidly into a nervous breakdown. I'm not going to stand around and let that happen. Besides which, if you don't go then your uncle won't feel comfortable in going, and that would be a real shame. He deserves a chance to get out and relax a bit.'

Mention of her uncle promptly made her feel guilty, as he had probably intended. Inwardly, Mollie flinched. It was true that Uncle Robert might decide against going, given the way he had been feeling lately, and she was most likely the only one who could persuade him otherwise. Drat Sam for making her think of that. She frowned. There had to be some way round the situation.

'You could go with my uncle,' she murmured evasively, 'and I'll perhaps follow later when I've finished the work.'

'And how are you planning to do that with your and still out of action?' Sam enquired grittily. 'Isn't that the reason I'm still accompanying you on visits?'

Her chin lifted. 'One of the reasons was so that

you could familiarise yourself with the area and with
the patients, but maybe it's time we should be thinking about doing things separately. I could probably
manage to drive myself around now.'

He shook his head. 'Oh, no, you don't. Not until
your stitches are out, and that will be another day or
so yet. As to this paperwork that seems to be both-
ering you so much, I'll help you out with it. End of
excuses.'

She slammed the drawer shut. 'We'll talk about it
later. Right now, I'm going to get some lunch and
deal with my morning's post. I can meet up with you
for the afternoon visits in, say, half an hour?'

It was a kind of a dismissal, and he didn't like it
at all. She could tell from the way his eyes hardened
like chips of flint that he wasn't finished with the
subject yet, but at least for the moment she managed
to make a dignified escape.

Their first visit of the afternoon was to Mrs
Lansdowne, mother of the boy who had suffered
from a bout of gastroenteritis last weekend.

'It isn't Richard this time,' Mollie explained as
they drew up outside the house. 'She called about
the baby. A rash of some sort.'

A tired-looking woman, aged around the middle
thirties, answered the door. Her hair was dark and
dull-looking, as though in need of a good brushing
and she wore a pair of faded jeans and a loose
T-shirt that hung shapelessly on her slender frame.

Mollie noted the faint lines of strain around the
woman's eyes and mouth. 'Hello, Mrs Lansdowne.
You called us about Stevie, is that right?'

'Yes, come in, both of you.' Jessica Lansdowne

stood to one side to let them into the hall. 'He's covered in a rash all over,' she said as they went into the living-room. She frowned, clearly worried. 'He's so tiny—he's only eight weeks old—and you don't expect them to get things so soon, do you? I took his temperature with one of those strips you put on the forehead, but he doesn't have a fever. He was one degree under what he should be. And he keeps being sick, bringing most of his bottle back up.'

'Let me take a look at him.'

'He's in his pram.' Jessica lifted the infant out and laid him across her lap. He squirmed restlessly, wailing crossly at the intrusion. 'That as well,' Jessica said. 'He's been crying a lot, really irritable.'

Mollie examined the baby, gently pressing a finger to an area of reddened skin. The colour blanched and then returned to the same degree of redness as before.

'Well, it isn't meningitis, I can reassure you about that,' she told the mother. 'With meningitis, the skin would remain discoloured when pressed, and that didn't happen. I think it's a simple virus that children do get from time to time, and nothing for you to worry about.'

She smiled down at the wriggling baby, and felt an unexpected tug at her heart. She had pushed aside thoughts of having a child of her own, but now, unexpectedly, she had visions of a tiny dark-haired infant nestled against her breast. Her throat closed, and she hastily blinked away the image, pulling herself together.

'He's gorgeous, isn't he?' she murmured huskily. 'And he certainly seems to be thriving, even though he's having a few problems at the moment. If he's being sick, you could try halving the amount of milk powder when you make up his bottles, just for the next day or so. Let him drink whenever he's thirsty.'

Jessica nodded, but something in her expression stirred an instinct in Mollie and prompted her to ask, 'Is anything else troubling you?' She waited, and when Jessica stayed silent, she added, 'How is Richard now? Is he over the stomach bug?'

'He's OK. Back to normal, up to everything that's going on, like all young lads his age. It isn't him I'm having trouble with. It's Tom that causes me all the hassle. I don't know what to do with him these days. He's changed such a lot. He's surly, and uncooperative. Won't eat. And then sometimes he sleeps in all morning, while other days he's just plain hyper.'

Sam's gaze narrowed thoughtfully. 'How old is Tom?'

'Sixteen. He's just left school, and it doesn't look as though he has any decent kind of future. No job to go to.' She sighed heavily. 'Not that it bothers him. He just dosses around the place, getting into trouble.'

'Sixteen's a difficult age,' he mused, 'and although he might seem brash about it on the surface, underneath it all he might be worried about not having a job. Have you tried talking to him about it?'

Jessica shrugged, settling the baby more comfortably in her arms and rocking him gently. 'It's hard to get through to him. He doesn't want to listen, and there's always an atmosphere. He doesn't get on with his stepfather, and there are rows.'

'And a new baby in the family,' Mollie put in quietly. 'We expect jealousy and behaviour problems with young children, don't we? But we imagine the older ones can cope without any difficulty. Perhaps you need to find a quiet moment when you're on your own to get Tom to talk to you without fear of reproach, just so he can tell you what he's really thinking.'

'And maybe go along with him to a job centre in the town,' Sam murmured. 'There might be a training opportunity of some sort that will appeal to him.'

'I suppose so. I've been so tired, lately, with the baby waking me up in the night. It's hard to think straight sometimes.'

'It must be difficult for you,' Mollie sympathised. 'The first few months with a new baby are always tiring. The only consolation is that it shouldn't last for too much longer. Perhaps you could catch a nap in the daytime to make up. Tom and Richard are old enough not to need watching every minute, aren't they?'

'You'd think so, wouldn't you? Maybe when Richard's back at school, when the holidays are over…' Jessica gave a weary smile and put the baby, now sleeping peacefully, back in his pram. 'Thanks anyway, Doctor. Thanks for coming. I'm glad there's nothing seriously wrong with Stevie. That would have been the last straw.'

They left Jessica a few minutes later, and began the drive to the next appointment. Inside the car it was hot, with the sun bearing down on them, and Mollie moved restlessly. Sam wound down the window to let in a draught of fresh air, but even so she felt overheated and wondered how much that was due to Sam's presence.

'I wonder if Tom sees anything of his real father,' he murmured, breaking into her thoughts. 'It didn't seem quite the right moment to mention him to Mrs Lansdowne but I'd like to know how many of his problems come down to anxieties on that score, especially since he doesn't get on with his stepfather.'

'There's not a lot we can do about it, anyway,' Mollie returned in a matter-of-fact way which belied her own frustrated thinking on the subject. One of the difficulties of the job was knowing when to stand back and simply let people find their own way. 'Maybe when she brings the baby in for his vaccinations I can talk to her a bit more.'

'That sounds like a good idea.' He turned the car into the country lane. 'Edie's next on the list, isn't she? Is she still having trouble with her chest?'

'I'm not sure. A neighbour rang and asked us to call in because she thought Edie wasn't herself. A bit confused, she said.'

They pulled up outside the house and Mollie knocked on the front door. She noticed that the curtains twitched before the door was finally opened and the old lady peered up at them, one hand holding onto the doorknob. Her grey hair was thinning, and Mollie saw that the skin on her arms looked dry and flaky.

'What do you want?' Edie frowned heavily. 'I told them from the Social I'm not going into a home.' She looked at Sam with suspicion and said fiercely, 'Who are you?'

'Don't you remember, Edie?' Sam said gently. 'I'm Dr Bradley. We came to see you on Sunday about your chest. Your neighbour, Martha, phoned the surgery this morning and said she thought you weren't well. She told you that we were coming to see you—do you recall that?'

Edie shrugged. 'Did she? Maybe. I think I fell asleep.'

'Can we come in, Edie?' Mollie asked. 'Just to make sure that you're all right. I promise you, no one's going to make you go into a home.'

Grudgingly, Edie opened the door, and they went through to the sitting-room. 'Don't know what all the fuss is about. No reason for Martha to go calling you.'

'She said you'd dropped something,' Mollie explained, 'and she was worried you might hurt yourself if you weren't feeling very strong.'

'Dropped something?' Edie looked vague. 'Did I?' She gave up the struggle for recollection, and added tartly, 'It's a poor thing if a body can't drop something without having folks get excited.'

'Maybe, but I think she was only trying to help. Have you had any problems with your hands or arms, Edie? Any weakness or loss of feeling? Any tingling?' Edie appeared to be moving about all right, but with the continuing confusion there was the possibility that she might have suffered a slight stroke, even though her speech seemed unaffected.

'No, nothing. I'm fine.'

'Good, I'm glad to hear it. But could I take a quick look at you, anyway, Edie? Your voice still sounds a bit croaky, so perhaps I should look at your throat first.'

The old lady allowed Mollie to examine her, and ran the stethoscope over her chest. 'That seems to be clearing up nicely, Edie. It might be that you're just a bit run down after your chest infection, though, and I think it might be a good idea to do a blood test, just to put my mind at ease that we're looking after you properly.'

Edie frowned. 'If you think so...'

Sam took the blood sample, while Mollie made a pot of tea, and they stayed and chatted with the elderly lady for a while longer.

Heading back to the surgery a few minutes later, Mollie said, 'I don't think there was much more we could have done right then, do you? She seems to be managing reasonably well, and she's feeding herself adequately, from what I can make out.'

He nodded. 'Just as well to check up, all the same.' He glanced at his watch. 'We've time in hand, so as soon as we get back I'll make a start on that paperwork you said was piling up.' He glanced across at her, wry amusement sparking in the depths of his eyes. 'Cinderella will go to the ball.'

She scowled down at her hands, the knuckles pressing into her lap. He was doing his utmost to make it difficult for her to get out of going to the barbecue this evening.

As it was, Robert was the deciding factor. He actually looked quite cheerful when they returned home, and he had already made a start on getting ready.

'Laura's picked a good day for it,' he said, fastening the buttons on his linen shirt. 'From the looks of things it should stay warm until late evening. Reminds me of the times when your aunt Becky used to put on a barbecue so the family could gathe

round, bless her. She loved to have everyone get together.'

'She did, didn't she? They were good times.'
Mollie smiled at him and touched his shoulder
gently.

'Laura's been wanting you to see her new house,
you know. You've always been busy up to now, but
she'll be glad you're coming along today at last.'

Mollie hid a wince. She couldn't let him down,
could she? Not when he was looking forward to
something for the first time in ages. It was pretty
clear that if she didn't go it would put a damper on
things for him.

Sighing inwardly, she acknowledged that she
would just have to grit her teeth and get through it
the best way she could. She ignored Sam's sidelong
glance. She could well imagine his enjoyment of his
victory.

Going upstairs to freshen up, she showered and
dressed, choosing a bright cotton top that fitted her
curves snugly and a pair of cream-coloured denims.
Her hair tumbled about her head in a riot of burnished curls, so she fixed it back with a pair of combs
and then finished off by adding a touch of lipstick to
bring colour to her soft, full lips. Finally, satisfied
that she looked all right, she went to join Sam and
her uncle downstairs.

They were talking, but Sam stilled as she walked
into the sitting-room, his eyes widening as his gaze
shifted slowly over her from head to foot. Her mouth
went dry under that lingering appraisal, and she
looked away, fussing unnecessarily around Robert

and making sure he had everything he needed for the short journey.

Sam drove them to the house, and when they arrived Laura embraced them warmly and embarked on giving them a swift tour of the place. Mollie swallowed hard and took a deep breath to try to contain her conflicting emotions. This was the home James and Laura had made together, but in other circumstances things might have turned out very differently.

There had been a time when Mollie had worn James's ring on her finger, and this might well have been her home. She pushed the thought aside and said evenly, 'It's beautiful, Laura. You've made it look perfect, homely and comfortable all in one. You must be very pleased with what you've done.'

'I am. Come on out on to the terrace and help yourself to a drink and something to eat. Everyone else is out there. I'll find Dad a seat near the barbecue—that'll please him.'

They smiled at that and went outside. So far there had been no sign of James, and Mollie was glad about that, though she wondered where he might be.

'Can I get you a drink?' Caroline's husband, Andrew, supplied her with a glass of white wine, and showed her the brick-built barbecue to one side of the patio.

'James's idea, apparently,' Caroline said. 'Purpose-built, and there for years to come. There's even a covered-in space underneath for grills and baking trays and what not. Now that's what I call planning.'

'I expect he has a cellar for the wine, too,' Mollie said with a smile. More friends came and joined them, and they caught up on gossip, nibbling on spiced meats and savoury rice and sipping at their drinks.

At intervals Mollie's gaze wandered across the terrace, and she caught sight of Sam, chatting with Laura. He looked powerfully masculine even in casual jeans and T-shirt, and she could understand why women found themselves wandering over to form a group around him. It wasn't just his looks. It was the way he listened, the way he made everyone seem special, his dry sense of humour.

She turned away, and tried to encourage her uncle to eat. His appetite was poor, and she was hoping the delicious food on offer would tempt him.

'I'm all right with what I've got,' he said. 'I'm fine.' But he didn't look fine, and she wondered if his earlier enthusiasm had tired him out. He seemed happy enough, though, talking to a friend from the local hospital.

'We're out of salad,' she murmured eventually, picking up an empty glass bowl. 'I'll go and see if I can find some more in the kitchen.'

The kitchen was modern, with neat cupboards, sparkling work surfaces and a large fridge-freezer to one side. She opened the door of the fridge, guessing that there would be extra salad in there.

'Mollie, you came, then. How are you? It's been a long time.'

Her heart stilled for a moment at the sound of that once-familiar male voice, but she had time to recover before she straightened up and turned to look at him. She even managed to collect herself enough to bring out a bowl of salad and place it on the table. Even more surprising, her hand was perfectly steady with no trace of a tremor.

'James. I wondered where you were.'

'I had to work late,' he said with a rueful smile. 'A business meeting that just went on and on.' A lock of fair hair tumbled across his forehead, making him look more youthful than his thirty-something years, and she remembered a time when she would have gently pushed it back.

It was strange how calm she felt. She had been putting off this meeting for so long, and yet now that it had come about she was more in control of herself than she could have imagined.

'How are things?' she asked.

'They're OK.' He came closer to her. 'I'm glad you came here tonight, Mollie. I've wanted to talk to you for a long time. I felt we never really said all the things we should have said, and I needed you to know that I'm sorry for the way things turned out. You never gave me the chance to explain properly.'

'There's nothing to explain,' Mollie said huskily, reaching for a tray and setting the bowl down on it. She busied herself, hunting around for tomatoes, and James reached out and caught her arm.

'Don't, Mollie,' he said. 'You've been avoiding me, but I want you to stop and listen to what I have to say.' He looked at her earnestly. 'I never meant to hurt you, you know. You were always my best friend. I cared very much about you. I always will, believe me.' He put an arm around her and drew her against him. 'We were so close before, and I didn't want things to end the way they did.'

She felt the air squeeze out of her lungs. She put a trembling hand up to his chest. 'James, I—'

'We're out of white wine.' The crisp tones sliced through the air like a knife, and Mollie jerked away from James and swung around to see Sam standing in the kitchen doorway. 'Laura said there was more in here.' He directed the words at James, but he was looking at Mollie, his eyes glittering like a cold edge of steel. She pulled in a beleaguered breath. James moved away from her as though he had been stung.

'I'll get some for you,' he said, recovering swiftly and going over to the wine racks which were set into the end unit.

He selected a couple of bottles and made to hand them to Sam, but Sam said coolly, 'Your wife is looking for you. I think it would be better if you took them to her.'

Had there been a slight emphasis on that word 'wife'? A nervous tremor ran along Mollie's spine, but she stayed her ground, her chin lifting. James looked uncertain for a moment, seeming to weigh the bottles in each hand, then muttered unevenly, 'Uh, right, yes, I'd better go and find her.' He glanced back at Mollie, adding, 'I'll catch up with you later, Mollie.' Then he went out into the garden, leaving her alone with Sam.

'Well, that was a cosy twosome I interrupted,' Sam said caustically. 'So now we know the truth of it, don't we? I can see exactly why you were so reluctant to come here tonight. You knew he would be here, and you knew you couldn't trust yourself to be in the same room as him, didn't you?' His voice was sharp with cynicism. 'Though I suppose I should give you some credit for trying to keep away, shouldn't I? At least you have some scruples.'

'I don't see that it's any of your business,' she responded tautly. 'Anyway, you don't know what you saw, not really, and you're jumping to conclusions.'

'Am I?' His mouth twisted in contempt. 'I saw you in his arms, I heard the gist of what he said to you. That was quite plain enough for me.'

Her mouth tightened. 'I don't have to explain myself to you. It isn't your place to tell me how to behave. My private life has nothing to do with you.'

He gave a harsh laugh, then raked his fingers through his hair. 'You're probably right about that. No wonder you didn't want me paying attention to you. Why would you when you're hankering after a married man?'

'It isn't like that,' she returned hotly. 'You don't understand—'

'I understand well enough that you were locked in an embrace with your cousin's husband,' he grated scornfully. 'Your cousin, for heaven's sake, who has been like a sister to you. How could you let it happen? What kind of a woman are you who could come between a man and his wife?'

'It didn't happen that way,' Mollie bit back, her temper rising. 'You only see one interpretation, and you think the worst.'

His eyes narrowed on her, taking in the fierce jut of her chin, the way her hands were clenched into small fists. 'He doesn't belong to you,' he said bluntly. 'You have to face up to that.'

She slanted him a long, hard look, her green eyes

smoky with warning. 'I'll decide what I have to do, how to live my life. I don't need you or anyone else to tell me what's right, or what isn't.'

She turned away from him, not wanting him to see that she was upset. What did he understand of the decisions she had made, the effort she made to steer clear of relationships that were ultimately doomed? He was a man, self-confident, assured, untouched by sorrow or pain. He couldn't possibly know what it was like to have your world come crashing down around your feet.

CHAPTER SIX

MOLLIE went back out onto the terrace and joined in with the general chatter among her friends as though nothing untoward had happened. Inside she was feeling churned up and unsettled, but she hoped it didn't show.

A minute or two later, Sam came out to talk to Robert and Laura, and she kept resolutely away from him.

When James approached her some half an hour later she was feeling more composed, and she said lightly, 'The house-warming's going well. Everyone seems to be having a good time.'

'They do, don't they?' He looked at her searchingly and said quietly, 'I'm sorry things were cut short back there. How are things with you, Mollie? Are things going well for you? From what I've heard, you've been too busy to take time out just lately, and I wondered if you were going to cut yourself off from us. I hope not—I didn't want to spoil things between you and Laura.'

'You didn't. I've just had a lot of work on, that's all.' She grimaced, and tried to put her thoughts into some logical form. 'Look, James, I'm happy for you that things turned out the way you wanted, really I am. Let's leave it at that, shall we? The past is over and done with, it's time to move on, and I do wish you well, truly.'

108

She felt better for saying it, as though a great weight had been lifted off her shoulders. Until now her feelings had been too raw, and she had tried to lock them away in a cold compartment in her mind and carry on as if everything was normal, pretend that she hadn't been affected in any way. She had even wished James and Laura happiness on their wedding day, but inside herself she had reflected on the deep irony of that. She had thought that love would last forever, but experience had taught her that you couldn't trust in love. Its fabric was too fragile, and at the first slight tug it simply fell apart at the seams.

'Enjoy your party,' she told James now. 'I'm going to see if there's any food left.'

The weekend passed quickly, with surgery on Saturday morning and medical literature which she needed to read up on in the afternoon.

She didn't see much of Sam because he went to check on the progress the builders had made at his house and then went to visit his parents on Sunday. Mollie wondered if he was purposely staying away. It was strange, not having him around, and she felt peculiarly disorientated for a while, but she fought off the feeling, throwing her energy into tackling the household chores.

Robert seemed to be battling with a chesty cough, and she was concerned that he had an infection.

'I'll give you some antibiotics to clear it up,' she told him, and he tried to argue that she was fussing, but didn't quite have the energy.

Going back to the surgery on Monday was almost a relief. She could lose herself in work, and she was doing something she loved. True, there were difficult times, but there were rewards, too, weren't there? Like being able to visit Jenny Ralston and her new baby boy. She decided to drive herself there, since her injured hand appeared to be healing nicely and wasn't giving her so much trouble.

It was late afternoon when she arrived at the cosy terraced cottage. Invited into the sitting-room, she peered down at the sleeping infant curled up on his side in his Moses basket and wrapped in a blanket. 'Oh, Jenny, he's such a lovely little thing. You must be feeling very pleased with yourself.'

'I am, definitely. He is a treasure, isn't he? Destroying all my beauty sleep with these three-hourly feeds, but there we are—there's no dealing with that.' Jenny beamed down at her infant son. 'We've called him Sam after Dr Bradley. Amy thinks that means Dr Bradley's the father so we're trying to put her straight before the rumours start flying around.' She grinned, and Mollie laughed.

'That would certainly leave him some explaining to do!'

Mollie left the house a few minutes later, after checking that all was well with Jenny. She planned on returning home to a relaxing shower and a meal she had left cooking on a low heat in the automatic oven, but her plans were short-lived.

Mrs Lansdowne called her on the mobile in a panic about twelve-year-old Richard.

'I don't know what's wrong with him. He's not been making any sense, and he kept falling over. Now I think he's unconscious. I'm really worried about him. Will you come and see him, Doctor?'

Mollie hurried over there, worried about what she might find. Jessica Lansdowne showed her into the sitting-room, where Richard was lying, unmoving, on the couch. Tom, the older boy, tall and lanky, with cropped hair, moved to one side as Mollie went and knelt down beside his brother. She spoke quietly to Richard, trying to get a response.

He mumbled incoherently, and she checked his pupils and pulse, then ran the stethoscope over his chest.

'What is it, Doctor?' Jessica asked anxiously. 'What's wrong with him?'

Mollie got to her feet and folded the stethoscope away in her bag. 'To be brutally honest, Jessica, I'd say he was plain drunk.'

Jessica looked horrified. 'You're not serious, are you? How can he be? We don't have any alcohol in the house.'

'I'm afraid I am,' Mollie returned steadily. 'He must have got it from somewhere.'

Jessica looked hard at Tom. 'What do you know about this?'

Tom looked aggrieved. 'Nothin', I told you.'

Mollie pulled out her mobile phone. 'He's going to need treatment, Jessica, because alcohol can have nasty effects on the central nervous system and might possibly cause difficulties with his breathing. The best place for him is hospital, where they can deal with all those problems if necessary.'

Jessica nodded, looking as though she was numbed by what was happening.

Mollie dialled the emergency number. 'The ambulance is on its way,' she murmured. 'In the meantime, I can give him something to encourage him to be sick, which will help a bit. Can you find a bowl or a bucket?'

Jessica hurried away and came back with a plastic bucket, which Mollie put to one side, ready for when the drug treatment began to work.

'He'll be given an intravenous dextrose solution at the hospital to combat low blood sugar,' she said, 'and he'll be monitored carefully, but it really would be helpful to know what he's drunk and how much.'

Jessica drew in a sharp breath and looked searchingly at Tom. 'If you know anything at all, Tom, I need you to tell me right now.'

White-faced, Tom looked at his brother, who was completely out of it on the couch. 'It wasn't nothin' to do with me,' he said fiercely. 'I think it was his mates—they nicked it from their dad's cabinet. Vodka or summat. About half a bottle.'

Mollie nodded. 'Thanks, Tom.' Turning to Jessica, she said, 'The ambulance should be here any time now. You might want to get a few things ready so that you can go with him. Will your neighbour look after the baby for you?'

Jessica nodded. 'I think so. I'll…I'll go and get myself sorted out.'

When the ambulance came Mollie supervised the boy's transfer into it and saw Jessica and Tom settled in beside him. 'I'm sure he'll be all right, Jessica. Try not to worry, he'll be in safe hands. I'll talk to you later.'

She watched the ambulance move away, and then went back to her car, wondering what would possess a twelve-year-old to down so much spirit in one go.

His friends, egging him on? She pulled a wry face. After this experience he might well decide to steer clear in future.

Laura was at the house when she returned home. Mollie walked into the living-room and saw Sam in there with her, sitting beside her on the settee. He was smiling down at her, a hand resting lightly on her shoulder.

Mollie stopped in her tracks. Clearly, they were getting on well together, and she wasn't sure how she felt about that. She didn't know what it was that bothered her about the situation, but her stomach made an uncomfortable flip and she had to make an effort to behave as though none of it mattered.

Sam's expression hardened as he saw her and she stiffened, determined not to let his coolness affect her.

'Hello, Laura,' she managed in a friendly enough manner. 'Did you stop by to check on Uncle Robert?'

Laura nodded but frowned, and Mollie noticed that she was looking a little pale. 'He's worse today, I think. He seems to have a bit of a cough, and it looks as though it's dragging him down. He looked haggard when I arrived this afternoon.'

Mollie bit her lip. 'I know. I made him start a course of antibiotics on Saturday because I think he has a chest infection, but they'll take time to get into his system. I still haven't had the results of the tests back, and I've been onto the laboratory to try to hurry them up. I don't know what's gone wrong there…short-staffed or something, I suppose.'

'I'll stop by again tomorrow to see how he is,'

Laura said, getting to her feet. She seemed weary, her movements slower than usual.

'Are you sure you're up to it?' Mollie asked with a frown. 'You don't look too well yourself.'

'I'm fine, don't worry about me.' She turned to smile at Sam. 'Thanks for looking after me. I appreciated it…and the tea.'

Mollie couldn't imagine how he had looked after her and decided that she wasn't going to ask, no matter how much the question niggled. Perhaps it was just that he, too, had noticed that Laura seemed under par. She might have been overdoing things lately, what with the new house and the job making demands on her.

A minute or two later she saw Laura to her car and waved her off, then went back inside to check on Robert for herself.

When she came back downstairs to the kitchen a short time later, Sam was checking the casserole in the oven. She said awkwardly, 'Will you do something for me?'

He looked surprised. 'What is it?'

She thrust her hand out to him. 'Will you take my stitches out for me? I'm fed up with having this dressing on my hand, and I think it's healed up well enough now.' It bothered her to have to ask him, but she couldn't manage the job on her own.

'OK. I'll do it now, if you like. The casserole will keep a while longer. Where do you want to go…bathroom, here?'

'Here will be fine.'

Mollie sat down by the table and he rolled up his shirtsleeves and set to work with the stitch-cutter, examining his handiwork with a professional eye. 'That'll be good as new in no time.' He added drily, 'You're lucky there was no lasting damage.'

She nodded and said ruefully, 'It's never a good idea to lose control. I don't usually react that way.'

'I dare say there were extenuating circumstances.'

She put her head to one side, thinking about that. 'A difficult man on the scene?' she suggested sweetly.

His mouth tilted wryly. 'That wasn't quite what I had in mind,' he answered, 'but perhaps that's what it takes to get through all the defence barriers you put up.' He sent her an assessing look. 'Did you take a piece out of James when your relationship came to an end? You were unhappy that things finished between you, weren't you? Did it come as a shock?'

She pulled her hand away from him. 'Which question do you expect me to answer?'

He lifted a brow. 'All of them?'

Her lips twisted in a brief grimace, then she said slowly, 'Breaking off a relationship is bound to be upsetting for both parties concerned, isn't it? When we were together I thought we had something special, and we were engaged for a time, planning to get married when I qualified. From the way things turned out, it seems it just wasn't special enough.'

He drew in a sharp breath, then said quietly, 'Can you tell me about it?'

Mollie stared down at her hand, looking at the line where the stitches had been. 'We met in a charity shop where I was working in the town. I was sifting through a box of books when he came in with a sack full of children's toys, just in time for Christmas. He stayed on and helped me sort everything out, and from then on we just seemed to click.'

She moistened her lips with the tip of her tongue. 'It wasn't long after Aunt Becky died, and he seemed to understand everything I'd gone through. He helped me through it, he made me realise that you can go on, and he made me laugh again.' She swallowed. 'I went away to medical school a few months later, and we got engaged one weekend when he came over to visit me. I thought we would marry after I had taken my finals.'

She looked up at Sam, sensing the tension in him, observed the taut sinews that corded his arms, the muscle that flicked in his jaw. 'There was a lot of studying,' she went on, 'and it was important to me that I should do well. I wanted a career that would be satisfying, and I wanted to be good at what I did.'

Her hands fluttered in a restless little motion. 'Perhaps that was where things started to go wrong. We spent such a lot of time apart, and maybe we didn't nurture the relationship as we should have. Anyway…eventually I found out that he had been seeing Laura.' She pulled a face, a grim little smile with no trace of humour. 'That was a conflict of loyalties I could have done without, on top of everything else.'

'I can imagine.' His eyes searched her face. 'It must have been hard for you to deal with that.'

She pulled in a shaky breath. 'I think Laura found it difficult, too. She hadn't meant it to happen—it started out as friendship, but I wasn't really surprised that he had fallen for her. She's sweet and attractive, everything that a man could want, I imagine.'

His eyes darkened, his smoky gaze moving restlessly over her pale features. 'Don't you know that you are, too? You mustn't let yourself be drawn into making comparisons.'

Gently, he drew her hand into his. 'Just because things went wrong between you and James doesn't mean that anyone is to blame. It's life, the way things are, and breaking up is just one of the hazards, one of the obstacles we have to negotiate. Staying the course and facing up to our mistakes is what makes us stronger as individuals.'

'I know that,' she said. 'It's just that I don't feel very strong right now, and I'm heartily sick of the obstacle race, so I've taken my name off the list of contenders. I want things to run smoothly from now on. I want to know what's ahead of me, and for that to happen I need to stay in control.'

His mouth twisted sardonically. 'Aren't you asking for the impossible? Is that why you've flung yourself into working all hours, so that you can opt out of real life? I told you before, you're a coward, Mollie. You're running away.'

His words caught her on the raw, but she wasn't going to let him see that they bothered her. 'You can think what you like,' she muttered. 'It works for me. I've learned to cope, and that's all that matters.' She moved away from him, feeling harassed. 'Thanks for seeing to my stitches. That feels a lot better… I must go and freshen up.'

She made her escape, but she was all too aware that she hadn't fooled him, and she felt the heat of his mocking gaze boring into her as she left the room.

When she came downstairs again Sam had removed the casserole from the oven and was serving it up. It smelled tantalisingly good, and she realised that she was starving.

'I've put some to one side for your uncle,' Sam said. 'He told me he didn't feel like eating yet. Is he looking any better?'

Mollie shook her head. 'No. You know, his condition has deteriorated since this cough started, and I'm beginning to wonder if his body can't cope properly with infection…if we're dealing with some kind of breakdown of his immune system.'

Sam nodded. 'I wondered that myself.'

Mollie stood by the table, lost in thought, and he said quietly, 'Sit down and eat. You can't do anything about it right now—we ought at least to give the antibiotics a chance to work before we start jumping to conclusions. And you should try to do justice to the delicious meal you've cooked.' He smiled at her. 'One of these days I must return the favour, but I can't promise you anything on a par with this. My culinary abilities are strictly limited to the grill and the microwave.'

She returned the smile, and sat down opposite him. They polished off the food and made coffee, and would have headed for the living-room, except that the phone began to ring stridently. They groaned in unison.

'I'll get it,' Sam said. 'You go and finish your coffee.'

He came back a minute or two later, his expression grave.

'What is it?' Mollie said anxiously. 'What's happened?'

'That was Edie's neighbour. Apparently, someone broke into the house and tried to rob the place while Edie was asleep. From all accounts she must have woken up and disturbed him, and he attacked her. It looks as though she has a head injury.'

Mollie stood up, her pulse quickening. 'Oh, no… Poor Edie. I hope it isn't serious.' She looked around for her medical bag. 'I'll go over there straight away. She must be in a terrible state, poor soul.'

'I'm coming with you,' Sam said. 'I want to see how she is. Do you think Mrs Baxter next door would keep an eye on Robert?'

She nodded. 'I'll go and ask.'

The police were there when they arrived at the house, and Sam stopped to speak to them about what had happened. Mollie hurried up the stairs and went through to the bedroom where Edie was lying on the bed, propped up with pillows. There was a nasty gash on her forehead, and blood had trickled down her face, matting her hair and spilling onto the bed linen.

'Edie, my love… How are you feeling? Can I take a look at you?'

'Wh-who is it? Was I sleeping?' The effort seemed to be too much for her, and Edie sank back against the pillows and closed her eyes. Mollie quickly examined her, looking for other signs of injury. She dressed the wound and watched her anxiously, concerned about her drowsiness and lack of memory about what had happened.

Sam came into the room as she was closing her medical bag.

'I think the head injury is the worst,' she said,

looking worriedly up at him. 'She seems to be concussed. We'll have to get her to hospital.'

'The ambulance is on its way.' He looked down at Edie, a spasm of indefinable emotion crossing his face. 'She looks so frail.'

Edie suddenly roused and began to heave, and Sam grabbed a bowl from the bedside table and brought it to her, sitting on the bed and supporting the old lady while she retched.

'How could anyone do something like this?' Mollie said huskily, her eyes bright with the sheen of tears. 'A defenceless old lady… It's just unbelievable that anyone could even contemplate hurting her.'

'The police think whoever did it was after money—for drugs, most likely. Her purse has been emptied—her neighbour thinks she had collected her pension this morning—and it looks as though savings have been taken from a cash box she kept in a cupboard.' His mouth tightened as he tried to contain his anger. 'They believe there might even be a link with the people who vandalised the surgery. They're not sure how many were involved here—Edie hasn't been able to say much about what happened.'

'I'm not surprised after what they did to her.' Mollie swallowed hard on a lump in her throat. 'I hope they catch up with them.' She rubbed the back of her hand over her cheek, dashing away a tear, and tried to pull herself together.

A muscle jerked along the line of his jaw. 'If it is the same people who broke into the surgery, I just thank heaven that you weren't there at the time. Who knows what they might have done to you?'

'I was all right,' she said quietly, 'and at least I have my health and strength—that's worth something. I could have put up a fight…and we have the alarm system in place now, which is more than poor Edie had.'

He said grimly, 'She had nothing to fight them with, nothing at all.' He got to his feet and went over to the window. 'I think I just heard the ambulance.'

The paramedics brought a stretcher and wrapped Edie carefully in blankets, before carrying her out to the waiting vehicle. Martha, the neighbour who had called them, hurried after them.

'I want to go with her,' she said quickly, looking anxiously at Mollie. 'She's very confused, and she might be glad of a familiar face later on.'

'I'm sure she will,' Mollie agreed. 'They'll probably do an X-ray, and I would expect them to keep her in at least overnight for observation, given her age and the severity of the blow.'

'We'll keep in touch,' Sam said. 'If she needs anything, let us know.'

They were both subdued on the drive home. Mrs Baxter greeted them and told them that Robert was sleeping, and seemed to be all right. After catching up on the news about Edie, she left them alone.

Mollie dejectedly pushed her bag down on the table and eased off her jacket.

'Are you all right?' Sam asked, watching her weary actions.

'Yes, I'm OK. I'll be better after I've had a good night's sleep, I suppose. Perhaps I'll have a shower and get ready for bed.'

'That sounds like a sensible idea.' He studied her

thoughtfully. 'I think she'll be all right, you know, after a few days' rest. We could go along to the hospital tomorrow and visit her, if you'd like.'

She nodded. 'Yes, I'd like that. I want to keep track of how she's doing.' It was thoughtful of him to offer to go with her, but she was beginning to realise that he was that kind of man, someone who could be relied on in times of trouble.

She went upstairs and showered as she had planned but, although she climbed into bed and turned out the light, sleep proved impossible. Instead, she lay there in the darkness, thinking about the events of the day and tossing and turning restlessly so that in the end she gave up trying altogether and decided to go and get a book to read from downstairs.

Slipping a robe over her cotton nightshirt, she went out onto the landing and immediately found herself in a collision with Sam. She gasped as her soft curves were crushed against his hard, lean body, and she registered the startling effect of the impact on her nervous system. She was all too conscious of the taut, muscled power of his thighs against her own, and the heated contact made the blood seem to sizzle in her veins and sent fierce, unbidden ripples of pleasure surging through every nerve fibre she possessed.

'Steady,' he murmured, his hands going to her arms as she swayed against him, her balance precarious.

'I'm sorry…' she managed huskily, her voice suddenly catching in her throat.

A faint smile pulled at the corners of his mouth

'You don't have to throw yourself at me, you know. I'll be a more than willing partner, any time you like.'

She opened her mouth to say something, but his hands were drawing her even closer, gently pressing her against the heat of his body, and everything went out of her head. He looked down at her, his blue gaze intense, thoroughly male, and his warm, knowing hands slowly began to stroke her supple curves, smoothing gently over the sweep of her spine. His tender, intimate caresses blazed a trail of fire over the rounded line of her hips, and all that came from her lips was a husky, 'Sam... I...'

'What is it, sweetheart?' he muttered thickly, his head lowering, his breath softly fanning her cheek. 'Can't you sleep?'

She shook her head, unable to think clearly for the swirl of heady sensation that clouded her mind. It was as though she had drunk too much wine. She was intoxicated by the feel of him, by the circling, hypnotic motion of those hands that made her pulse leap in frantic urgency and coaxed her body to a trembling response.

'I came out here to...to get something,' she whispered raggedly.

His eyes glittered, sparks firing in the blue depths. 'What was it you wanted...? Will I do instead?' Amusement curved his mouth.

'You're laughing at me,' she protested huskily, her hands shakily pushing at the solid wall of his chest. She felt the warmth of his skin beneath her palms, and her fingertips tingled in response.

'Would I do that?' he murmured. His glance ran

over her, touched the fiery mass of her hair and slid down over the creamy curve of her shoulder, slowly explored the outline of her slender shape. She heard the swift intake of his breath, and realised with a sense of shock that her robe had fallen loose.

His lazily sensual gaze lifted, coming to rest on her flushed face. Flame sparked in his eyes and he muttered thickly, 'I was never more serious.' Bending his head towards her, he said against her cheek, 'You're such a delightful temptress, soft and warm and inviting. You make it so hard for me to resist you.' Then his mouth touched hers, and the warm, coaxing pressure of his lips stole every thought from her mind. She absorbed the sweet thrill of that kiss, startled by the shattering explosion of sensation that spread through her veins like molten honey.

Her body meshed with his in reckless abandon, excitement pulsing heatedly through her veins. She felt his hard strength stir against her, and wondered fleetingly if she should draw back, now, while there was still time.

'I want you, Mollie,' he muttered, his voice roughened. 'If you only knew how much I want you. You're like a fever raging inside me, burning me up.'

Didn't she feel it, too? He was talking about want, and she recognised all too well that it was passion which was driving him. But was that enough? What about love? Shouldn't there be love? Without that wouldn't it all fall apart?

Her mind cautioned her, but her body had a will of its own. She wanted his kiss to go on and on, she revelled in the feel of his arms around her, holding her safe, protected, keeping the world at bay.

How could he do that? An inner voice sounded scornfully in her head. Wasn't it just an illusion, an ideal scenario that didn't exist? Wasn't love just a fantasy? He had said himself that she was asking for the impossible.

'Mollie?' His hand found the fullness of her breast, his thumb circling the tingling nub, and she gave a shuddery sigh, aching to respond to the sweet invitation but at war with herself.

She shook her head, and looked up at him, the breath snagging in her throat. 'I'm confused,' she said in a choked voice. 'I'm not ready for this, I need time to think...'

'You don't need to think,' he muttered huskily. 'Why cloud the issue? Just go along with what you feel, give in to what your body's telling you.'

'I can't. It won't work, I know it won't...' She pulled away from him and turned towards her room. 'I'm sorry.'

A brooding darkness came into his eyes. 'I was right, wasn't I?' he said, a taut edge to his voice. 'You'd rather creep away and hide from life than face up to what it has to offer.' His mouth tightened. 'You can't bring yourself to experience any basic emotion that might jerk you out of that cold little prison you've built around yourself.'

Mollie pulled in a sharp breath. '"Basic" was your word,' she threw back. She would have said more, but she thought she heard a sound from Robert's room at the far end of the corridor and she stopped to listen. Perhaps he was waking.

'It's apt enough,' Sam muttered tersely. 'You daren't allow yourself to feel anything.'

'It was just sex,' she said in a tight whisper. 'That's the "basic" you were looking for. You're just angry because you missed out. You wanted to get me into bed, and now you're mad at me because it didn't go as you'd have liked. Well, I'm sorry about that, but that's just too bad. If you can't take the heat, maybe you should go and take a cold shower.'

'There's nothing wrong with sex,' he tossed back. 'You should try it some time.'

'I don't need advice from you.'

'Don't you?' His eyes hardened, a dangerous glint like that of steel shimmering in their depths. He moved closer. 'You may think you're safe in that icy little cocoon, but you've forgotten that ice has one major flaw in its make-up. Sooner or later it succumbs to meltdown. And when that time comes, sweetheart—' his voice smoothed to a silken drawl '—I plan on being around.'

Her confidence faltered under the onslaught of his steady gaze, but she fought back bravely. 'Don't bank on it,' she retorted under her breath, backing towards her room.

Whether he would have followed she never found out, because just then there was another sound from Robert's room, a low, pained groan, and after that there was a crash and the sudden shattering of glass.

Sam turned at the same moment she did, and they ran together to the room at the end of the corridor.

CHAPTER SEVEN

ROBERT was lying on the floor amongst the broken remains of a glass jug which had been on his bedside table. Mollie looked at his slumped body in horror, and ran over to him.

'Uncle Robert, can you hear me?'

He mumbled something that she couldn't catch, and she turned to Sam, saying quickly, 'Help me lift him. We must get him back on the bed and find out what caused his collapse.'

'I'll do it.' His glance moved swiftly over her as she stooped by her uncle's side, and his brows drew together in a dark line. 'Come away from the glass or you'll injure yourself again.'

'I think he's cut himself,' she said, distraught. 'He's—'

'They're superficial, from the looks of things,' he said briskly. 'Move out of the way, Mollie. Go and get your medical bag.'

His sharp tone made her lift her head in shock, but she recognised the sense in what he was saying and she ran to fetch the bag, returning within a couple of minutes.

By that time Sam had Robert back on his bed, and he had already made a brief assessment of his condition. 'His pulse is slow and I think he's dehydrated,' he said quietly. 'He's in a bad way. I need to check his blood pressure, but I think we'll find it's fallen dramatically.'

He put the pressure cuff around Robert's arm and took the measurement, then glanced across at Mollie. 'It's dangerously low,' he muttered, confirming her worst fears. 'He needs to be in hospital. Call an ambulance, and we'll do what we can here and now while we wait for it to arrive. I'll give him a shot of hydrocortisone.'

She frowned, her mind working busily. 'Are you thinking the same as me?' she asked. 'Are we looking at Addison's disease?'

'Could be,' he said grimly. 'They'll need to do a test to confirm the diagnosis at the hospital, but everything seems to point that way, given this collapse and his symptoms over the last few weeks.' He pulled open the medical bag and drew out a syringe.

Mollie stirred herself and phoned for the ambulance. If they were right, it meant that Robert's adrenal glands weren't functioning properly, and his body couldn't produce the hormones that were vital to his survival. They had to be replaced, and the hydrocortisone that Sam was injecting could help to save his life.

'We need to replace the fluids he's lost,' she said raggedly. 'I'll get some saline and glucose from the emergency dispensary downstairs.'

They set up an intravenous line, then started to investigate the extent of his cuts from the glass. He fingers shook as she bent over her uncle's still form and tried to tend some of his wounds. 'How could have let this happen?' she whispered. 'If I hadn' been out there on the landing with you—'

'Pull yourself together,' Sam said sharply. 'Stop blaming yourself for something that isn't your fault.'

'I might have got to him sooner,' she argued. 'I could have stopped him from falling.'

'You couldn't have stopped his collapse,' he said, his tone gritty. 'You need to stop thinking that way and concentrate on doing what you can to get him through this. He needs you now, more than ever, clear-headed and clear-thinking. There was no way you could have known what was wrong. All we know is that this collapse must have been building up over the last few weeks, and now we have to deal with it as best we can.'

He was right about the way his illness had been building up, she acknowledged heavily. Uncle Robert's condition had been slowly worsening over some time, and now he had suddenly been precipitated into a crisis situation.

'The chest infection must have been the last straw,' she muttered hoarsely. 'His body simply couldn't cope.'

Sam checked Robert's pulse and blood pressure again, and then listened to his chest. 'There isn't much more we can do for him until the ambulance arrives.' His eyes narrowed on her. 'You'd better get dressed if you want to go with him.'

She was suddenly angry. 'Of course I want to go with him.' He was talking to her as though she were a child—issuing commands, telling her how to think—and it rankled, spurred her into action.

When she came back into the room, clothed in jeans and a sweater, she was a little calmer. 'I should have thought of Addison's before,' she said huskily.

'If I'd put two and two together I might have been able to help him sooner, prevent all this from happening.'

'It's a rare disease, not something you would automatically think of,' Sam returned abruptly. 'Besides, there's no tell-tale darkening of the skin in the creases of his palms or in his mouth. You had no reason to suspect it.'

She stared unhappily at her uncle. 'I don't know what could have caused it,' she muttered. 'It looks as though his immune system has stopped working properly, as though his adrenal glands have been damaged in some way—'

'We won't know anything for some time,' Sam remarked briskly, 'and sometimes no one ever knows the cause. Stop tormenting yourself over something you can do nothing about.'

She flinched at his harsh tone. He didn't know what she was feeling. She dealt with sick patients every day, but it was never like this, never this hard to bear. It was different when it was one of your own family, someone you loved dearly, someone who had been like a father to you—that made it so much more painful. How could he possibly understand?

She stayed quiet, though, after that, doing what she could for her uncle, working with Sam until the ambulance arrived.

'We'll see to him for you,' the paramedics said, gently moving her to one side. 'You go and get your things.'

In a daze she did as she'd been bade. Sam went out with her to the ambulance and helped her to climb inside and seat herself alongside Robert. When they were ready to go she saw him standing in the road, watching them, and wondered why he wasn't coming with her. She needed him to be with her. Then the doors were shut and they started the half-hour journey to the hospital. She held her uncle's hand and felt numb inside.

The doctors were ready for them when they arrived at the hospital. Robert was rushed straight into Casualty, and a team set to work on him. Mollie was left standing to one side, unable to do anything except watch. Only then did she begin to feel the full weight of what was happening. She felt lost and alone, and tears welled up in her eyes.

'You can't do anything here, Mollie. Sister's offered us her office—let's go in there and get a coffee.'

She looked around and saw Sam through her blurred vision, her throat dry and aching. 'You came,' she said. 'I didn't know—I thought you had stayed behind. Oh, Sam, I'm so glad you're here.'

She felt a rush of relief swamp her, and when, after a moment's hesitation, Sam put his arms out to her she went into them, burying her head in the hollow of his shoulder.

'I thought it best to follow on in the car,' he murmured against her hair. 'You weren't thinking too clearly, but I knew you would need someone to be with you and take you home later.'

She gulped down a broken little sob, and nodded against his shirt-front. 'Thank you for coming.' His warmth and solid presence comforted her, and she slowly absorbed strength from him.

After a while, in a more subdued frame of mind,

she straightened and dabbed at her face with her fingers.

'We should let Laura know,' she managed quietly.

He nodded. 'We'll use the phone in Sister's room. She won't mind.'

Laura and James arrived within the hour, and Mollie tried to explain what had happened as best she could. 'He's very ill,' she said, 'but they're doing everything they possibly can for him.'

Laura began to cry quietly. Mollie put her arms around her and felt the shudders that racked her cousin's slender body. She hugged her close, wishing that she could take away some of the heartache.

'How soon will we know if he's going to be all right?' Laura asked after a while, and Mollie bit her lip, searching for an answer.

'It's hard to say, Laura. First of all the consultant needs to confirm the diagnosis, and then it all depends on how well Uncle Robert responds to treatment. It will probably be at least twenty-four hours before we know much more.' The consultant in charge wasn't the one they had been waiting to see, but at least they were in a better position to confirm a diagnosis now.

Laura moved restlessly, her fingers twisting in the fabric of her skirt. 'I feel so helpless, so useless.'

'We all do right now. The waiting's always the worst, but he is having the best treatment he could possibly get.'

James came and put his arm around his wife, supporting her. 'The doctor said that Mollie and Sam could well have saved his life, by being there an treating him on the spot. We have to be thankful for that.'

Mollie watched James as he tried to comfort Laura. He walked with her to the side of the room and coaxed her to sit down, holding her when she would have jumped up again in agitation.

'It's all right, I'm here, we'll get through this together,' he murmured softly. 'He's always been a strong man up to now, Laura. He won't let this get the better of him, you'll see.' He stroked her hair and soothed her, and Mollie looked on and felt fresh tears sting the back of her eyelids. She turned away and saw that Sam's gaze was fixed steadily on her, his eyes dark and brooding.

She lifted her chin. Back at the house he had said that she needed to be clear-headed and clear-thinking, and he was right. She would be no good to anyone if she gave in to self-pity and self-doubt. People looked to her for support, and she needed to set an example.

She glanced down at her watch and registered with a sense of shock that it was nearly seven in the morning. 'I didn't realise that we had been here most of the night.'

'We have surgery in a couple of hours,' Sam said. 'I don't think we can cancel at this late stage, but I'll see to it on my own if you want to stay on here. I don't think you'll see any change in him for some time to come, though.'

'You go if you want, Mollie,' Laura said quietly. 'We'll stay on for a while, and we can let you know if anything happens.'

Mollie hesitated but sensed that Laura wanted to

be alone with her father for a while. 'All right.' Her throat was painfully tight. 'I think I'll feel better if I'm doing something, if I can keep myself busy.'

Sam took hold of her arm and led her to the door. 'The hospital has our number, so do Laura and James. If anything happens, they'll let us know.'

They went home and freshened up, taking time to eat a quick breakfast before making a start on the surgeries. Their lists were both full, and Mollie found it peculiarly ironic that life seemed to go on in the same old way, no matter what happened to individuals.

She put on a professional front and did her best to deal with sore throats and abscesses, and prescribed creams for rashes, and was thankful nothing major cropped up. By midday she had seen the last of her patients and she went along to Reception, where Sam was looking through a bundle of patients' notes.

She paced distractedly across the room until Sam looked up and said, 'Why don't you go and get some lunch?'

'I'm not hungry.'

'You need to eat something to keep up your strength,' he commented tersely. 'You'll be no use to anyone if you allow yourself to fade away.' He tossed down the bundle of notes. 'You could probably do with getting away from the surgery for a while.'

She frowned. 'There isn't time to go back to the hospital, is there?'

'Not if we're to be back in time for the afternoon appointments. We can do the visits together and head for the hospital after that.'

'I suppose you're right. I feel so inadequate,' she said shakily, 'having to stand back and let the hospital staff get on with it.'

She started to pace again and Sam stood up and came over to her, putting his hands on her shoulders and gently kneading them with his thumbs. 'Try not to feel too badly, Mollie,' he said. 'You've taken care of him, you've always been there for him, and that's what counts above all else.'

'It doesn't seem enough,' she muttered distractedly. The warm pressure of Sam's hands on her arms and the rhythmic circling of his fingers was comforting, soothing away some of her inner tension. She didn't seem able to think straight.

'It is.' Slowly, he released her, and for an odd moment she felt a peculiar sense of loss before she pulled herself together. She walked over to the reception desk and began to leaf through her post.

'Leave that,' Sam commanded. 'Caroline's already sifted through it to see if there's anything urgent. You need a break.' He reached for his jacket. 'Come and have lunch with me at my house. I could do with checking up on things there.'

'I suppose I could,' she said doubtfully. 'How far away is it?' She had to admit to a certain curiosity about the kind of place Sam would have chosen, and she wondered how the builders were getting on with the renovations. If they were near to finishing, it could mean that Sam would be moving out of their place shortly, and she wasn't sure how she felt about that. Somehow, over this last couple of weeks, she had grown used to having him around.

'It's about a mile from here, backing onto fields

close to the river and the weir. The workmen won't be there today—an emergency job cropped up—so we'll have the place to ourselves. We can stop off at the village store on the way and I'll buy lunch.'

Mollie nodded. 'OK. I'll get my bag.'

His house was large and rambling, she discovered, brick-built with ivy-covered walls and large Georgian windows, set back from the road and screened by silver birch trees, as well as oak and sycamore. She could see at once why he had chosen to live here. It was beautiful, a jewel in the middle of a sweeping rural landscape, and as they approached the wide front porch the sun cast its rays over the walls of the house and touched them with a golden, welcoming warmth.

Sam took her inside and showed her around, and she saw that the interior was just as impressive. The rooms were spacious, and created such an impression of comfort and perfect simplicity that it was clear that Sam had impeccable taste. In the lounge, the furnishings reflected a deep-seated warmth and an eye for colour and design that made her catch her breath.

'This is beautiful,' she murmured. 'It's so large and full of light.' Her gaze took in the full-length windows and glazed doors opening out onto a paved area overlooking the garden. Beyond that she could see fields and rolling hills in the distance, and the river winding its way to the sea. She turned to him in awe. 'Oh, I could live with that.' Then she realised what she had said, and coloured slightly. 'I mean—'

'I know what you mean,' he said, his mouth curving. 'I'm glad you like it. Come and let me show you the rest of the house.'

They went upstairs, peeking into the bedrooms and main bathroom, and then went into what must be the master bedroom. Again the window was large and looked out onto a curving expanse of lawn, bordered by shrubs and trees. One of those trees had a swing fastened to its thick branches, probably left there by the previous owners, and there was another with a rope ladder dangling from it. It all added to her impression that everything about the house was perfect. It was warm and inviting…a family house. Strangely, the thought disturbed her.

She turned away from the window, conscious at once of Sam's tall figure beside her, aware of his powerful masculinity, of his strength. Right at that moment it was an immense comfort to her.

'It's such a lovely view from here,' she managed huskily.

'I think so,' he murmured.

Distractedly, she peered into the annexe and looked around, and he pushed the door open wider so that she could see properly.

'I'm having this bathroom redecorated,' he said. 'There's still the tiling to be finished off in here, but at least the new shower cubicle is in place.'

'I'm very impressed with it all,' she said simply. 'It's a lovely house. You must be very glad you found it.'

'I am,' he said with quiet satisfaction. 'I've always admired this house from a distance, and I couldn't believe my luck when it was put up for sale.' He took a last glance around, then he became brisk once more. 'Let's go downstairs and eat, shall we? I'm starving.'

They went into the kitchen, where the light oak units reflected the sun's rays in mellow golden tones and the burnished copper canopy glowed brightly over the hob. 'It looks as though most of the cupboards have been fitted,' he said, 'but the island bar's still to be put in place and as yet there's no oven. Everything's coming on nicely, though.' He glanced down at the packages they had bought for lunch. 'Shall we eat outside? It seems a shame not to be in the sunshine.'

She stepped out onto the terrace and sat in one of the garden chairs by the table, looking out over the garden. They ate fresh bread with cheese and salad, and slaked their thirst with a pitcher of fruit juice.

'This is a family house, isn't it?' Mollie said, after a while. 'I can imagine it filled with children.'

'I dare say my young nephews and nieces will enjoy it,' Sam said, a wry shape to his mouth. 'Especially if they get to see the ducks on the water beyond the fence.'

'That's why you've kept the swing and the rope ladder,' she guessed with a faint smile. 'You must be very close to your family.'

'I am. I've had to keep in touch from a distance up to now and make do with occasional visits, but I feel as though I'm at the stage where I can put down roots at last.'

'Do they all live and work around here?'

He nodded. 'My parents are both retired now. My mother taught infants at the local school, but these days she's glad of the time she can spend with her grandchildren.'

'And your father?'

'He worked in a laboratory, doing pharmaceutical research. My brother has followed in his footsteps, but my sister gave up her work to be a full-time mother. She thought hard about it because she had a good career in nursing and she didn't particularly want to give it up, but I think she's doing the right thing. Her children are still only toddlers, and they need to be with their mother. All children need the security of the family, don't they? Especially in the early years.'

Mollie swallowed hard, fighting against a sudden tremor of indefinable emotion that welled up in her. 'I'm sure that's true,' she said huskily. 'She'll be able to watch them growing up, and she won't have lost anything because in a few years' time she will probably be able to go back to nursing.'

Sam reached for her hand and she was dismayed to find that it was shaking. 'I'm sorry,' he said quietly, stroking her fingers lightly with his thumb. 'That was thoughtless of me. I didn't mean to upset you. I should have thought it through before I spoke.'

She shook her head. 'There's no need to be guarded around me.' She attempted a smile. 'I'm quite grown-up now. I had a secure childhood, at least in the early years, and when I lost my parents...' she made a helpless little gesture, trying to fight off the memory '...I was at least old enough to understand what was happening.'

'That makes it worse somehow, doesn't it?' he said with a frown. 'At twelve years old you're growing up fast, and you're particularly vulnerable then, when you're trying to come to terms with all the physical changes that are going on in your life. That's the time when a girl becomes particularly close to her mother.'

'I had my aunt.' Mollie smiled wistfully, recalling Aunt Becky's sweet, gently lined face. 'She was a lovely woman. I couldn't have asked for a better, more loving person to take care of me. She always treated me as if I were her own daughter.'

Sam's eyes narrowed thoughtfully. 'How old were you when you lost your aunt?'

A lump seemed to swell in her throat. 'Eighteen. It was very sudden, really. She seemed to be well enough, except for some bad headaches…' Her voice faltered. 'Then one day she had a stroke, and that was it.'

He winced. 'That must have been rough for you.'

'It was rough on all of us, especially Laura, but we just had to carry on as best we could.'

She stared blindly out at the garden, then said in a cracked voice barely above a whisper, 'What am I going to do if I lose Uncle Robert as well? Sam, I don't think I could bear it.'

She turned to him, pain obvious in the wavering line of her mouth and the shimmering green of her eyes. 'Why does it keep happening to me?' she asked despairingly. 'Why do I always lose the people I love? It's getting so that I daren't let myself care deeply for anyone. In the end it's too painful, there's too much hurt.' She bent her head, battling to stem the tide of tears that threatened.

Sam reached for her, his hands cupping her face

his thumb tilting her chin so that she had to look into his eyes. 'How can you say that you can't care for anyone? Didn't you go into medicine so that you could make a difference in people's lives? Think of all those babies you've brought into this world, the sick and the infirm you've helped to a better life.

'You can't tell me that you don't care about them because I know that you do. I've seen it in the things you do on a daily basis, and I know, even after spending just a short time working with you, that the people around you love you and want you to be part of their lives.'

He stroked her cheek lightly, running his thumb along the line of her cheek-bone. 'Don't feel crushed because things get hard. There's always another day just around the corner when things won't look quite so grim, and you should reach out and grab hold of life while you can. There's joy in simply being alive, Mollie, in being with the people who care about you.'

He took her hand in his and squeezed it lightly. 'Promise me you'll keep your chin up, that you won't let things get you down.'

She managed a weak smile. 'I'll try,' she said huskily.

They went back to the hospital later on that afternoon, and found that a ward round was in place and the team were gathered around Robert's bed.

'You may as well go and get a drink or something,' the nurse said. 'Give them half an hour, and then you can go and see him. There's little change as yet but he's no worse, which is good.'

'Thank you.' Mollie looked at Sam. 'If we can't

see him yet, I could at least go and see Edie while
we're here. I rang up this morning and she hasn't
been discharged yet, so it might be a good time now
to go and see how she's doing.'

'We'll both go. Come on.'

He led the way along the corridor to the lift, and
they went to the reception desk to find out Edie's
whereabouts.

'Her condition stabilised and they transferred her
to Ward 12,' the duty receptionist told them.

Mollie was taken aback. 'But that's a geriatric
ward,' she said, frowning. 'What is she doing there?'

The receptionist gave a light shrug. 'You'll need
to take that up with the registrar, I imagine.'

Mollie nodded. 'I will.'

The registrar was in another part of the building,
but the house officer was in Sister's office, dealing
with a call regarding a new admission. When he had
finished, he said pleasantly, 'I'm Dr Wilson. What
can I do for you?'

'I understand you've transferred Edie Fernley to
the geriatric ward,' Mollie said. 'She's a patient of
mine. I'm Dr Sinclair, the GP who admitted her. Can
you tell me why you think she's geriatric?'

Dr Wilson consulted Edie's case notes. 'Ah, yes,
slight fracture to the skull... That's not causing too
many problems, though, of course, there was some
swelling, and there's a good deal of bruising. On the
whole she's doing all right, but she does appear to
be very confused and, frankly, Dr Sinclair, it was felt
that she is suffering from a form of dementia. We
are, of course, doing everything possible to see that
she's comfortable.'

'As her GP, I don't have any reason to believe that she's suffering from any form of dementia. In fact, I—'

'I'm sorry, Dr Sinclair, but I did talk to the registrar on duty, and it is our considered opinion that she needs to be treated for that condition. The neighbour who came with her confirmed that the old lady had been increasingly confused at times before the attack. I know it's upsetting, and there will be difficulties, of course, because I understand that she was living alone at the time of the assault, but we feel that the situation isn't at all satisfactory. We shall have to liaise with Social Services and try to arrange some other form of accommodation when the time comes for her to be discharged.'

'I know that she was confused at times,' Mollie said, a glint of determination coming into her eyes, 'but I did a blood test recently and sent it for analysis. I received the results this morning, and it appears that she has a thyroid condition. Her thyroid is under-active, and that could give rise to the symptoms she's been displaying. I agree that it might look like dementia, but I think you'll find that her condition will improve considerably if she's treated with thyroxine.'

Dr Wilson blinked. 'Thyroxine. Ah… Perhaps we should look into that.' He frowned down at his notes. 'I'll speak to the registrar about it, Dr Sinclair.'

'Thank you. In the meantime, I'll go and see how she is. I shall keep in touch.' Mollie headed off down the ward in search of Edie.

'That was good thinking, getting the blood test,'

Sam said. 'You must have had an idea of what was wrong.'

'I knew she wasn't herself so I took a guess at the likely cause.' She pursed her lips. 'It's just upsetting that I couldn't do the same for Uncle Robert.'

Edie seemed to be recovering from the assault physically, but she wasn't very clear who they were or why she was in hospital. They stayed with her for a while, and Mollie did what she could to put her mind at rest.

'I hope they find whoever did that to her,' Mollie said grimly when they came away. 'It makes me so angry, just thinking about it.'

'Hold onto that anger,' Sam said. 'It's a good, cathartic emotion.'

They went back to Robert's ward, and found Laura at his bedside.

'He's still not very responsive,' she told them. 'The nurse said he needs as much rest as he can get, so we shouldn't try to disturb him.'

'Have you been here all day?' Mollie asked.

'No. I went home for a change of clothes and to get something to eat. James had to go to work,' Laura added wearily. 'Did you speak to the consultant?'

Mollie shook her head. 'I haven't had the chance. I'll go and see if I can find him.'

'Do you want me to go?' Sam offered.

'No, I'd sooner hear what he has to say for myself.'

'All right. If you're sure.' Sam pulled up a seat at the side of the bed beside Laura, and Mollie went in search of the consultant.

'It's definitely Addison's disease,' Dr Hastings

told her. 'It can take months, or years, to develop, and it is quite rare so you have nothing to blame yourself for, not picking up on it. Until such time as there is a crisis, like now, diagnosis can be difficult. However, I think we've managed to stabilise his condition, and we'll keep him under observation for the next few days. After that, of course, he will need to be on steroids for the rest of his life.'

'At least now we know what it is we can do something to safeguard him,' Mollie said quietly. 'Thank you, Doctor.'

She went back to the ward, and saw that Sam had his arm around Laura. Their heads were together and they were engrossed in an intense conversation, from what Mollie could make of it, and when they finally became aware of Mollie's presence they sprang apart guiltily. She didn't think he had simply been comforting her.

She came to an abrupt halt, stunned by the feelings of anger and raw jealousy that rose in her. What was going on here? What was Laura doing, getting close to Sam? All at once she wanted to rage at both of them, but she struggled to rein in her violent emotions, taken aback by the sheer force of her reaction. She didn't want to see Sam getting close to another woman, and especially not with her cousin. And yet what right had she to complain when she had consistently pushed him away?

As rational thinking returned, she bit back the sharp comments that had come racing to her lips.

'Did you see him?' Laura asked.

Mollie tried to compose herself. 'Yes. It's Addison's disease. He'll need a lot of nursing care while they try to replace the hormones his body can't produce.' She made an effort to keep calm and stop herself from voicing her doubts about the pair of them. This was hardly the time to raise questions, was it, when they were waiting anxiously around her uncle's bed, and anyway appearances could be deceptive, couldn't they?

Even so, it had looked very much as though they had been caught out being secretive, but why? Surely Sam couldn't be thinking of starting a relationship with Laura, could he? After the way he had railed at Mollie for being in a close embrace with James, it would have been the height of hypocrisy, wouldn't it? Her stomach knotted painfully. Up until now she had respected Sam's integrity without question. It was heart-rending to think that he might no longer deserve that respect.

Yet she couldn't get it out of her head that this wasn't the first time she had seen them in a secret huddle, and the knowledge that they were hiding something from her hurt badly, more than she would have thought possible.

She went and sat down beside Robert's bed and held his hand, trying not to think about Laura and Sam. 'Keep your chin up,' Sam had told her, and she would do that, even if she was crying inside. She wouldn't let them see that she cared.

CHAPTER EIGHT

MOLLIE struggled through the next few days. They passed in a muddle of visits to the hospital and trying to fit in work at the surgery, as well as dealing with a number of call-outs. The surgeries were as busy as ever, but at least they kept her mind from straying to problems that couldn't be resolved.

Lee Simmons came in with his mother for a check-up, and when Mollie ran the stethoscope over his chest she was pleased to find that it was clear.

'That's brilliant, Lee. Better than it's ever been. You're doing very well.'

'I thought you'd say that,' the five-year-old said with a pleased grin. 'And I've got some news for you,' he added proudly, his eyes wide. 'My mum's given up smoking—' He stopped to look at her open mouthed reaction, then went on, 'She weren't half bad-tempered, but she done it.'

Mollie's glance flew to his mother, and Mrs Simmons confirmed it with an eager nod. 'He's right, I did. I was a horror to live with,' she added with a little laugh. 'I admit it... But I made up my mind, and now I've done it. I can't tell you how pleased I am with myself.'

'That's wonderful news,' Mollie said with a smile. 'The best I've heard all week.'

When they were ready to go, Mollie gave Lee a smiley sticker for his T-shirt, and then, in a moment

of mischief, pressed one to his mother's cotton top
as well.

'I think you deserve one, too,' she said with a grin.

Lee's face lit up like a beacon. He nodded. 'Well
done, Mum,' he said in a tone that was sweetly pa-
ternal. 'You've been a very good girl.'

They both went out smiling, and Mollie felt her
spirits lift a little. At least two people were happy.
She just wished she could hear some good news
about Uncle Robert. It was hard to think of him lying
there, looking so ill.

'Are you bearing up all right?' Sam queried when
they had finished for the day. His gaze narrowed as
he tried to read her expression.

'I think so,' she said quietly. 'It helps to be able
to keep working, to keep myself busy. There's less
time to dwell on problems.'

'Perhaps he'll have had a change for the better
when we go along to see him today.'

'I hope so.' She glanced at him, her expression
serious. 'Thank you for being with me through all
this, for going with me to the hospital. It would have
been so much harder to cope with everything on my
own.'

His eyes were dark and unfathomable. 'You only
have to ask, Mollie, if there's anything at all that you
want. You can rely on me.' His mouth made a faint
spasm. 'Besides, I've come to think of Robert as a
good friend over these last few weeks. I want to see
him get well as much as you do.'

He went with her to the hospital again that evening, but Mollie was disappointed to discover that
there was no real change in Robert's condition. He

slept most of the time they were there, looking oddly helpless, and every so often a nurse would come and check his drip or take his pulse.

Laura was there, too, watching him anxiously whenever he stirred. Once, when he groaned faintly, she put her hand to her mouth, and Sam said gently, 'You can't read anything into the way he is right now, Laura. He's holding his own so far, and all the signs show that at least he's stable.'

Laura nodded, but some of the colour had drained from her face and Mollie thought she didn't look too well.

'Are you feeling all right?' she asked. 'You look a bit pale. Is there anything I can get for you—a cup of coffee or something?'

'No, thanks. I'm fine,' Laura answered huskily. 'I've just had a long day, that's all. I thought I'd tackle some re-upholstery and try to renovate the conservatory furniture while I have the house to my-self.'

'Is James away, then?'

Laura nodded. 'Yet another conference.' She pulled a face. 'These business meetings seem to have taken up more and more of his time just lately.' She sounded thoroughly fed up, and something in her tone and general manner made Mollie wonder if the problem went deeper and whether, perhaps, her mar-riage might be in trouble.

It was worrying if that was the case, Mollie re-flected, and it was odd, but she didn't feel any of the conflicting emotions she used to experience when-ever she thought about James and Laura. She frowned. Her feelings for James had dissolved completely, and now she just thought of him as a friend.

James was a good man, and he probably thought he was doing the best for their future by working so hard. Laura, on the other hand, seemed concerned that he was away from home so much.

'Why is he having to put in so many hours?' she asked.

Laura shrugged. 'According to him, technology's advancing so fast they have to keep on top of things, and that means endless overtime to sort everything out.'

She grimaced, and Mollie tried to sympathise. 'Your furniture stands to benefit from his absence, anyway,' she murmured, trying to lighten things a fraction.

That night, though, when she was lying in bed, she thought about what Laura had said. She had been unhappy lately, that had been clear, but Mollie didn't think it was only because her father was ill. There was more to it than that. She was feeling low because James was away, and she probably needed support of some kind, especially at this difficult time.

Had she turned to Sam for that support because he was a good listener, because he seemed to care? Had she turned to him for more than that? Mollie's stomach churned as she fought off a sudden wave of nausea. How could this be happening? Why, when she was just beginning to open her heart to Sam, did it all have to turn to ashes?

Mollie spent a restless night, and when she looked in the mirror next morning there were shadows under her eyes which had her reaching for her make-up bag. She made repairs to her face, adding a dusting of blusher to her cheeks, and then finished off with a touch of lipstick. After a minute or two she decided that she was up to facing the world. Thank heaven it was Saturday, and there would only be a short morning surgery.

Edie's neighbour was the last patient on her list. Mollie looked up from her notes and smiled at her.

'Martha, how are you? That rash isn't back again, is it?'

'I'm afraid it is.' Martha looked rueful, and showed Mollie her reddened throat and chest. 'I think you were right when you said it was to do with my nerves. I suppose I got all het up over Edie being attacked, and the hospital and everything, and now I'm covered in blotches again.'

'Oh, dear. Did the cream I gave you last time do any good?'

'Yes, it did, but I used it all up.'

'I'll give you some more.' Mollie entered in the details on the computer. 'It was a very upsetting business, wasn't it?' she added as she printed out the prescription.

'I still haven't got over it,' Martha agreed, her fingers twisting spasmodically in her lap. 'I double check the doors and windows every night, and I still get nervous, wondering if whoever did it will come back. You never know, do you?' She grimaced. 'I've been trying to put Edie's place straight for her over the last few days because I didn't want her coming back to that mess…and then I felt awful after I heard they wanted to make her go into a home. There have been murmurs about it before, and she was always worrying about it. Can they do that to her?'

'I don't think it will come to that, Martha. Last time I phoned the hospital Edie was feeling much more like her old self, and I'm pretty confident that she'll be able to come back to her own house.'

'Oh, that is a relief.' Martha smiled. 'I'll make sure she has some flowers about the place to welcome her back.' She looked much more relaxed now, and when she left the room a few minutes later her step was visibly lighter than when she'd come in.

Mollie switched off her computer and tidied her desk. It was good to know that Edie had a neighbour who cared enough to look out for her, she reflected as she headed for Reception.

Sam came out of his room and checked through the post in his tray, a frown pulling his brows together, and she went and sat on a corner of the table and watched him.

'Problems?' she asked. 'Did you have a difficult morning?'

He looked up at her. 'Nothing I couldn't handle. John Framley was bitten by his dog and had a nasty wound. I managed to stitch him up OK and I gave him a course of antibiotics, but he was more upset about the dog than anything else. Didn't know what had caused him to turn on him like that.'

Mollie winced. 'What is he going to do about it?'

'He's not sure. He'll have a word with the vet probably to see what the best course of action would be. It could be that the dog's old and in pain and was trying to warn him off.'

'At least that might turn out to be something treatable.'

'I suppose so.'

'How are things otherwise?' she asked. 'Are things going well at the house? You've been so busy lately, between visiting your family and coming to the hospital with me, I don't suppose you've had much of a chance to keep track, have you?'

'It's all finished,' he said. 'In fact…' he wafted a letter in front of her '…this is the final invoice from the builders for the work that was done.' He looked at the figures on the paper and gave a mock grimace. 'Looks as though I'll need to find work on the night shift to pay for it.'

Mollie was instantly concerned, and he gave her a wry smile, seeing the look on her face. 'Don't worry about it. I'm just kidding.' He pushed the invoice back into its envelope. 'But it does mean that I can move my things out from under your feet over the next day or so and give you room to breathe.'

'The next day or so?' Mollie echoed.

His brows met. 'This evening, if you'd prefer. It was just that I've some deliveries being made over the course of this week. I had some furniture in storage, and there are lots of bits and pieces at my parents' house that I need to collect, but—'

'No, no…take as long as you need,' she said hurriedly. He was going so soon? 'I've liked having you around,' she confessed. 'I'd sort of got used to you being there and having someone around to sound off at every now and again over this and that. It will seem strange without you.'

His glance flicked over her, but his eyes were dark

and she couldn't make out his expression. He said evenly, 'Once Robert is back home you'll have plenty to occupy you. He'll be glad of your company. It's time I moved into my own place.'

His cool, faintly abrupt manner took her aback a little, though she didn't know quite what kind of reaction she had expected. Perhaps, deep down, she had hoped that he might have wanted to stay with her, but that was foolish thinking, wasn't it? He had his own life, his own interests, and she was the least of them.

She didn't reveal anything to him of what she was thinking. That would have exposed too much of her inner self and have left her open to ridicule, so instead she murmured, 'If that's how you feel.'

'It is. It's for the best.'

She said diffidently, 'If you need any help with the move, I can always lend a hand. I know there's bound to be a lot of upheaval, and toing and froing, so if there's anything I can do just shout.'

'Thanks.' He gave her a brief smile. 'I expect I shall need plenty of help with all the unpacking. Actually, I was going to make a start this afternoon.' He glanced at his watch. 'I picked up some bits on my way here, so I might as well go straight over there and get organised.'

'I'm not doing anything this afternoon,' she said quickly. 'I planned on visiting the hospital this evening, but I'm all yours for now if you'd like.'

His mouth looked wryly cynical. 'You'd probably like to rephrase that.' His brows lifted, and his eyes glittered as he scanned her features.

Warm colour ran along her cheek-bones as she

realised what she had said. 'Yes…well…you know what I mean.'

'I probably do,' he said, a sardonic edge to his voice. 'I think you may have put me straight on that score once or twice.' He stood up, dropping his post into a tray. 'But thanks for the offer. I'm sure I'll be glad of your help so, if you're ready, we may as well go now.'

She worked alongside him at the house, first of all hanging curtains in the lounge. Then she went into the kitchen to unpack crockery and cutlery from cardboard boxes and find a home for them in his cupboards.

'It looks beautiful in here now,' she said, looking around appreciatively. 'They made a good job of everything.' She found a set of pans in the box on the table and searched for a place to put them.

'I'm pleased with it,' he murmured in agreement, his eyes holding a satisfied gleam.

Mollie bent to stack pans in one of the units, then she straightened, pushing a stray tendril of hair from her cheek.

His glance moved over her. 'You're looking a bit flushed. I've obviously been working you too hard. I think maybe it's time we stopped and had something to eat. I'll see what I can rustle up.'

He peered into the fridge and produced a wedge of cheese, along with tomatoes, ham and butter. 'Cold fare, I think. I should have some crusty bread somewhere, if I can remember where I put the bread in.'

She laughed and went to help him find it. 'It was on top of the microwave last time I looked.'

He shook his head. 'I can't imagine what it's doing there.' He dived into the fridge again and brought out a bottle of chilled white wine. 'I think we might drink a toast to my new home.'

She cast an uncertain glance over the bottle. 'We're still on call this afternoon, you know,' she reminded him. 'I doubt the patients will appreciate it if we turn up the worse for wear.'

His eyes glinted with amusement. 'If that were to happen, I'm sure they wouldn't blame you. I'm the newcomer around here so they would probably come to the conclusion that it's all my fault, that I'm the one who's leading you astray. I expect there'll be gossip all around the village about the new doctor trying to get their sweet and delectable Dr Mollie into his dark clutches.'

'Fool,' she said tartly. He was making fun of her, and she didn't want him to think he was getting to her with his provocative remarks.

His mouth quirked, his gaze slanting over the pink flush of her cheeks, and he murmured silkily, 'You might scoff, but these things happen, you know.' He uncorked the bottle and paused momentarily, a gleam of mischief flickering in his eyes.

A rush of heat threatened to invade her whole body, and with a huge effort of will she struggled to dampen it down. Keeping her tone as even as she could manage, she said, 'And what about drinking and driving? Aren't you bothered about that?'

His mouth twitched, but he poured wine into two crystal glasses and said smoothly, 'This wine is barely alcoholic, just a light, sparkling, fruity drink to add zest to the meal.' He handed her one of th glasses. 'So, you see, you'll be quite safe in my hands. Unless…' Blue eyes met hers and lingered for a disturbing moment. 'Unless, of course, you'd prefer it otherwise?'

Her eyes widened, and the breath caught in her throat. His light-hearted manner flustered her, and she didn't know how to respond just then. Of course, he was only teasing her and looking for a reaction, and perhaps the best course was to stay immune. It just meant getting a grip on herself, that was all. She attempted to send him a quelling glare but failed miserably and, instead of being chastened, he laughed softly.

He was irrepressible, she decided, and would have turned away but he clinked their glasses together in a toast and said, 'Good health and happiness, Mollie.'

'And to you.' She returned the toast, her gaze meshing with his, but this time she couldn't read the expression in those dark blue depths and she quickly looked away, sipping slowly at her drink to hide her confusion.

He said calmly, 'It looks as though—'

He didn't get to finish what he was going to say, though, because there was a sudden loud banging on the door and at the same time the bell rang and above it all they heard children shouting.

Sam frowned. 'I'd better go and see what that's all about.'

She followed him out to the hall, glass in hand, and watched while he opened the door.

'Will you come and help us?' A boy of about twelve or thirteen said the words in a rush, his face

pinched and anxious-looking. 'Someone's in the water.'

'We can't reach him,' a girl put in. 'We don't
know what to do.' Her thin body was shaking, agi-
tated, and she was ready to run back the way she had
come.

Mollie put her glass down on the hall table. There
were three of them altogether, and the other boy was
in an equally distressed state.

'Will you come? Now?' The girl's eyes were
pleading, wide and frightened.

'Of course,' Sam said. 'Calm down, and tell me
exactly where he is.'

She pointed to the fields at the back of the house.
'In the river, down by the weir. We were messing
about and he lost his footing and got swept away.
Hurry, please.'

Sam was already on the move. A cold shiver rip-
pled through Mollie's body, but she acted quickly.
'I'll get my medical bag,' she told Sam. 'You go with
them and do what you can. I'll follow.'

She ran to get her medical bag and emergency
equipment from the boot of her car, along with a
couple of travel blankets she kept in there. By the
time she was ready, Sam was already running along
the path which led from the back of the house towards the fields and the river.

She found herself praying that they would get
there in time, and when she reached the river she
could see more children on the bank, their faces
white and shocked, their eyes fearful.

Her glance went quickly to the water, and she
made out the figure of a boy. Oddly, he was swim-

ming towards the weir, struggling against the current, and he looked exhausted, as though every stroke was an effort. Then her heart filled with dread when she realised that he was trying to reach another smaller figure further along. The water flowed in a torrent, bubbling and churning restlessly, and where it gushed over the weir it frothed and sent spray shooting into the air.

Sam was stripping off his sweater, his actions swift and precise. He kicked his shoes off onto the grass at the water's edge and dived in as close as he could get to where the smaller figure bobbed in the water.

Mollie looked around to see what she could do to help. A gnarled old tree spread its boughs over the river, and she ran up to it and started to pull at one of the thicker branches, urging the children to come and help.

'This branch might be long enough,' she muttered. 'If we can break it off we might be able to hold it out to him.'

They pulled with her, and at last it made a cracking sound and they managed to tug it down. Mollie ran along the bank to the part of the river where the younger boy had drifted, and tried to reach him, shouting for him to grab the branch, but he didn't seem to hear her calls. He was being buffeted this way and that by the surge of the water, and she was desperately afraid that they were too late to save him.

Sam was swimming strongly, his powerful arms propelling him through the water towards the child. Mollie waited, an agonised, dreadful wait, and then Sam reached him, was holding him up in the water and battling against the swirling current to bring him to the side.

Mollie dropped the branch and put her arms out to help lever the lifeless child out of the water and up the bank onto the grass.

'Can you look after him?' Sam asked briefly, his breath coming in short bursts. Water plastered his hair to his scalp and ran down his face. His clothes clung wetly to his strong body. 'I need to find the other boy. He's gone towards the weir.'

'Yes, I can manage.' Her attention was on the child at her feet, and she dimly registered that Sam had gone back into the water again.

She worked on automatic pilot, concentrating her attention on the child who was sprawled, unmoving, on the grass. She recognised Richard Lansdowne, and her eyes filled with tears as she looked at him and saw that his face was tinged with blue-grey and his chest was still, with no sign of rise or fall.

As she knelt down beside him she said huskily to the children who had gathered around, 'Has anyone gone to fetch his mother?'

A tall, dark-haired boy answered. 'Jamie went.'

'Good. One of you use my phone to call an ambulance. It's in my bag, on the grass.'

She carefully tilted Richard's head back and checked inside his mouth, gently moving his tongue out of the way. Reaching for her medical equipment she quickly brought out a guedel tube and used it to keep the airway clear. Then she put the mask of the ventilation bag in place over his mouth and nostrils and started to squeeze the bag, getting oxygen into his lungs.

'Can you do this for me?' she asked the dark-haired boy, who was standing beside her.

He looked taken aback, but nodded.

'Good. I need to check his circulation.' She felt for the carotid pulse at the side of Richard's neck, but there was no sign of one and she quickly started cardiac compressions, in between showing her helper what to do. 'Give him time to exhale between breaths.'

She tried desperately to start the boy's heart. 'Come on, Richard, do this for me,' she whispered. 'Breathe for me. You must.'

There was movement at the side of her, and she glanced up briefly to see Tom Lansdowne, soaked through, exhausted and deathly white.

He sank down beside her. 'It's all my fault,' he said brokenly. 'I should have stopped him. I was supposed to be looking after him.'

'Don't blame yourself, Tom,' Mollie said. 'You tried to get to him, to save him.'

'I didn't, though. I didn't get there in time, did I?' He broke off, then said in a voice little more than a thread of sound, 'Is he going to die?'

Mollie didn't answer, concentrating on compressions and checking whether Richard was breathing.

'It's all my fault,' Tom said again, tears beginning to stream down his face.

'There's a blanket over there, Tom. Go and put it 'ound yourself,' Mollie said.

He shook his head. 'I'm not leaving him,' he said iercely.

There was more movement beside her, and this ime it was Mrs Lansdowne who dropped to her knees beside the child. She started to rock backwards and forwards, whispering his name over and over again.

Water trickled out of Richard's mouth and Mollie held her breath, waiting, then continued with the compressions. There was more water, then he coughed, and Mollie's heart lifted.

She felt for his pulse again, and it registered faintly beneath her fingers. His chest began a slow rise and fall, and when he coughed again Mollie said a heartfelt prayer of thanks.

'Is he going to be all right?' Tom's tone was urgent, but Mollie, watching Richard's struggle to focus his eyes, waited.

'Richard,' his mother said. 'Richard, I'm here. Can you talk to me?'

'Mum?' He looked at her, and she gently squeezed his hand.

'I'm here, it's all right.'

'I'm sorry, Mum.' He closed his eyes, and Mollie reached for a blanket and quickly wrapped it around him. She was afraid his body temperature would drop, and she didn't want him to go into shock.

'Richard?' His mother's voice was desperate. 'Don't you give up on me now.'

'I'm sorry, Mum,' he said again hoarsely, trying to concentrate his attention. 'I know you said we shouldn't play around here.'

She hugged him to her, her eyes brimming with tears. 'You're safe now. That's all that matters.'

Mollie felt overwhelming relief flood through her. She sat back on her heels and looked at the boy who had been helping her with the ventilation bag. He looked very pale, and his hands were trembling.

'You did very well,' she told him with a smile. 'You helped save his life. Thank you.'

She watched Tom and Richard with their mother, and thought they all needed a minute or two alone together.

'I'll fetch another blanket,' she murmured, getting to her feet and walking over to the grassy slope a few yards away, taking time to breathe deeply and calm herself.

There was no sign of Sam, and she frowned, sweeping a glance over the meadow and surrounding hedgerow. Where was he? With both boys out of the water, she would have expected him to be here with them. What could have happened to him?

Going back to the family, she knelt down and wrapped the remaining blanket around Tom. Richard was still pale, but he had lost the blue-grey tinge and she felt confident that he had suffered no long-term damage.

Mrs Lansdowne had recovered a little from the shock, and said sharply to Tom, 'Where were you? Why weren't you looking after him?'

'I was, to start with,' Tom tried to explain, 'but these boys came by, and I had to see them about something.' He stopped, and for a minute it looked as though he was going to be sick. 'I was only going to be a little while. I told Richard to keep away from the water and said I'd be back in a bit. I didn't think he would go in, honest, Mum. He hadn't got his swimming things with him, just his shorts, and I thought it would be all right.'

'It wasn't, though, was it?' His mother's face was tight with strain. 'He might have died, and all because you went off with those so-called friends of yours. I don't like those people you've been mixing with. They're nothing but trouble.'

Tom looked ashen and was beginning to shiver, and Mollie was worried that shock was setting in. She wrapped the blanket more firmly around him and put her arms around him, chafing his back with the palms of her hands to warm him.

'The ambulance should be here soon, Tom. The paramedics will take you both to hospital and make sure that you get warmed up and see that you recover from this without any harm.' She looked over at Richard. 'Are you feeling better now, Richard?'

He nodded, leaning back tiredly in his mother's arms.

'Good. It won't be long now.'

Mollie turned back to Tom and asked quietly, 'Did Dr Bradley get you out of the water, or did you manage on your own?'

'He grabbed me and pushed me up onto the bank. He told me to get out onto the grass. He said Richard was over here.'

'Did he get out of the water with you?'

Tom looked perplexed. 'I thought he did.' He looked around, and his frown deepened. 'I thought he followed me. I wanted to get here to see if Richard was all right, and I didn't look back.' He stared at her, realisation dawning. 'Do you mean—do you think he might still be in the river?'

Mollie swallowed painfully, and her lips were quivering as she spoke. 'I'm beginning to think tha he might be. I can't see him anywhere around, can you?'

Shakily, she got to her feet. 'I have to go and see if I can find him. Stay here, and keep close together to keep warm. Do you think you'll be all right for a few minutes?'

Mrs Lansdowne nodded. 'You go and I'll look after these two. We'll shout if we need you.'

Mollie started to walk back towards the river, heading for the weir. Why wasn't Sam here with them? She couldn't stop the sudden trembling in her limbs, and there was a cold feeling of dread in the pit of her stomach. Had he slipped back into the water, too exhausted to get out?

Her mind rebelled at the thought. He had to be safe. He had to be, because what would she do if she lost him? How could she go on?

CHAPTER NINE

WHERE was Sam? Mollie ran along the side of the river, searching frantically for any sign of him. He had to be here somewhere. He couldn't just have disappeared without trace, could he?

There was no sign of him, though, and she stared down at the churning water near the weir and found herself praying again, praying that the violent, seething depths held no dark secrets.

'Sam...where are you?' she called out in panic, rushing farther along the water's edge, apprehension growing inside her with every minute that passed.

'Please, Sam, answer me...' There was no clue as to what might have happened to him, and she was beginning to despair.

Her glance scanned the far side of the river, skimming the trees and the hawthorn bushes and coming to rest on a wooden bridge further downstream. Was something moving near the bridge, or was it just that her eyes were playing tricks on her?

She was already hurrying off in that direction. As she drew nearer to the bridge she stopped and looked over there again, putting a hand up to shield her eyes from the sun.

She saw the figure of a man, and her heartbeat quickened. He was on the bridge, walking towards her and as she came closer still she recognised the strong, muscular body and relief surged through her.

'Sam, where have you been? What happened to you? I was so afraid.' She ran to him and hugged him, and at first he seemed to register faint surprise, then his arms went around her and she felt his muscles tighten as he held her in a firm embrace.

The wetness of his clothing seeped through her cotton outfit, making the thin material cling damply to her breasts and thighs, but she didn't care. She hugged him closer, crying into his chest.

'Hey—what's this all about, Mollie? What's wrong?' He tensed suddenly. 'Richard... Is he—?'

'I think he's out of danger,' she managed, her voice wobbling. 'Tom seems to be OK.' She sniffed and tried to control herself, but the tears kept on coming, and he cupped her chin and tilted it so that he could see her face. Through a blur of tears she saw that there was a gash on his temple, and her fingers came up to examine the wound.

He held her wrist, stopping her. 'Tell me what's upsetting you so much.'

She banged on his chest with her free hand. 'What do you think's upsetting me? Don't you know? I thought I'd lost you. You disappeared and I had no idea where you were. I thought something dreadful had happened to you and I was just so scared—'

She started crying all over again, and he swept her up against him, holding her tight, kissing the salt tears from her cheeks and teasing her lips apart so that she had no choice but to stop mumbling and crying and kiss him back, measure for measure. His kisses tasted sweeter than anything she had ever known, like the water of life, filling every crevice of her being and making her whole again.

When at last he released her she stared up at him, dazed, her thoughts scattered on the breeze. Nothing seemed to matter any more, except that he was here with her, safe.

When she thought that he might have gone from her life, she knew without any doubt that she couldn't bear to be without him. It was simple, really, and she should have recognised it before, except that she had been afraid to acknowledge her feelings. She loved him.

Anything that had gone before was nothing compared to what she felt now. She had never experienced anything like this. She wanted him, body and soul, for ever and ever, but...but there had been so much hurt in her life already. How could she risk laying herself open to more?

In the far distance there was the sound of an ambulance siren, and she felt as though a draught of cold air had descended on her. Life was such a fragile thing—in the last hour or so there had been ample evidence of that.

'We must go back to them,' she said. 'Richard seems to be all right, but he needs to spend a night in hospital in case there are any complications after his ordeal. I think Tom's simply exhausted, emotionally and physically.'

'He's not the only one, from the looks of things.' His blue eyes searched her face intently as he supported her, an arm at her waist. They started back towards the trio.

'Is it any wonder, after you went missing like that? What happened to you?' She looked at the matted wound on his head. 'How did you do that?'

'I lost my footing after I helped Tom out of the water. I slipped back into the river, and I must have knocked my head on a branch or something. Anyway, I was dazed for a bit, and when I recovered I found I was over on the far side of the river. It was easier to climb out over there and make my way back via the bridge.'

She drew in a quick breath. 'You might have drowned,' she said huskily. 'We weren't there to help you out. We didn't know what was happening.'

He looked down at her worried face. 'Don't you know I come from a line of strong-bodied octogenarians?' He smiled at her. 'We're a tough breed, we Bradleys. It would take more than a few knocks to keep one of us down.'

A shiver ran through her. 'You were certainly lucky this time.'

She frowned as they drew nearer to the Lansdownes. Mrs Lansdowne's voice was raised, and Mollie wondered what was wrong. Tom and Richard looked well enough after what they had been through, but they were both quiet and looked white and drained of energy.

'Tom, I want to know what you were doing with them,' Jessica Lansdowne was saying. 'I told you to keep away from those boys, but you wouldn't listen, would you? Was it drugs—is that what you were after?'

'No, Mum, honest, I don't do them any more. That's the point. I was trying to finish with all that. That's why I had to meet them, to tell them. I wasn't going to have anything to do with them any more.'

'I don't believe you,' his mother said. 'How can I believe a word you say?'

'It's true.' Tom sounded distressed. 'It was after what happened to Mrs Fernley. I wouldn't have nothin' to do with that. It was wrong, she was just a nice old lady, and they shouldn't have done that.'

Mollie's step faltered as she reeled in shock at what she had heard, and Sam's arm tightened around her instantly, steadying her. When she had recovered they walked silently over to the small group and she went and sat beside Tom on the grass, while Sam checked that Richard's condition was stable.

'Tom,' Mollie said, 'do you know something about what happened to Edie?'

He nodded, looking shame-faced and miserable. 'It wasn't anything to do with me. These people I know, they wanted money for drugs and they didn't care how they got it. They thought it would be easy, just break in and grab whatever they could find.'

'If you didn't have anything to do with it,' Sam said, 'why didn't you go to the police?'

Tom shrugged awkwardly. 'I was scared. I didn't know what to do.'

'Were they responsible for the damage at the surgery as well?'

He nodded. 'I swear it was nothin' to do with me. I know I should have said something, but I didn't know who to talk to.'

His mother said sharply, 'You could have talked to me or Martyn.'

'What could you have done?' Tom threw back 'You would have just got upset and angry, and

Martyn would have lost his temper and shouted at me. He's not my real dad, he doesn't care about me.'

The ambulance siren had stopped, and Mollie could just make out the vehicle on the main road at the far side of the field. A group of children was waiting there, by the field gate, to show the paramedics the way.

'Of course he cares about you.' His mother's expression was shocked. 'You don't give him a chance, do you? You just go around with a big chip on your shoulder, blaming him for being in the house instead of your dad. How do you expect to get on with him if neither of you makes an effort? You have to at least try to like him.'

'Why should I like him? He's not my dad. He shouldn't try to act as if he is, telling me what to do and what not to do.'

Jessica sighed, and put an arm around Tom's thin shoulders. 'I know it's been hard for you, but Martyn really does want to be friends with you. He sees you getting into trouble and he wants to help, but you keep pushing him away and then he gets angry and frustrated. We'll talk to him about all this together, and we'll sort it out between us. But you have to make an effort to get along with him. Will you try?'

Tom squirmed uncomfortably, looking down at his fingers and twisting them together. 'I suppose so.'

The paramedics arrived with a stretcher and organised Richard's transfer to the ambulance, along with his mother and brother. Both boys were wrapped in heat-retaining blankets and seemed to be bearing up well enough, and Mollie stood by the doors, watching as they were settled in.

'You'll be OK now, boys. They'll check you over at the hospital, and get you warmed up.'

Mrs Lansdowne said quietly, 'Thanks, both of you, for all you've done for my boys. I'll always be grateful to you.'

'I'm glad they're safe,' Sam said.

'So am I.' She made a wry face. 'I'll talk to Martyn about this business of the break-ins, and I'm sure he'll do what he can to sort it out at the station. I expect Tom's dad will want to handle most of it, though. He's been working away these last few months, trying to get enough money put by to start his own business, and we haven't seen much of him. I think he'll come back now, though, when I tell him what's happened.'

They watched the ambulance drive away, then walked slowly back towards Sam's house. Mollie was subdued and saying very little, and Sam's gaze narrowed on her.

'What are you thinking? Are you worried about them?'

'I think they'll be all right, physically,' she said quietly. 'Emotionally, though, there are a lot of scars that will take time to heal. It can't be easy when families are broken up, especially for the children. It must be so difficult for the parents, trying to decide what to do for the best. I wouldn't want to put any child of mine through that.'

'Have you thought about having children of you own?'

She shook her head, trying to ignore the empty place inside her that cried out to be filled. 'I ju

don't think it will work out that way for me. There
are too many obstacles in the way.'

His eyes darkened. 'Things change. You might not
always think like that.'

'It's how I feel now.' They had reached his house,
and she said with a frown, 'You ought to get changed
out of those wet things. Do you have any spare
clothes here?'

'No, I don't. Shall we go back to the cottage?'

'I think that might be a good idea, and I'll have a
look at that gash on your head.'

At the cottage he went upstairs to shower and
change into dry clothes, and she used the time to heat
up a pan of vegetable soup. He would probably be
glad of a hot meal, and it was the best she could
come up with in a short time.

When he came downstairs again he was wearing
fresh jeans and a sweater, and he looked so good she
had to resist the urge to go and put her arms around
him. She was still smarting from the shock of the
afternoon and all she wanted was to hold him close,
but she wasn't sure how he would react. Besides, he
was hurt.

Instead, she said quietly, 'Let me take a look at
the wound on your head.'

It was deep and ragged, and he probably had a
nasty headache as a result of the knock he'd received,
but he wasn't saying anything about it. She put in a
few stitches to tidy it up, and when she had finished
she said, 'You should have some antibiotics to ward
off any infection, after being in that water.'

'Maybe.'

'I've made you some hot soup,' she told him. 'Eat

up and it will help to counteract the chill of your soaking.'

'You didn't have to do that,' he said, but all the same he sniffed the air, savouring the appetising smells coming from the cooking pot. 'Not that I don't appreciate it, of course.'

He sat down at the kitchen table and she ladled soup into a bowl. 'It's the least I can do,' she murmured. 'I don't know what I would have done without you these last few weeks. You've helped me through all this worry over Uncle Robert, and you've been a godsend at the practice.'

His brows lifted, and he banged the flat of his hand to his ear and then shook his head as though it was waterlogged. 'Am I hearing things properly? Is this the same woman who, not so long ago, told me I wasn't needed around here?'

She had the grace to blush at that, but she said airily, 'I've mellowed. I really do appreciate all that you've done.'

He leaned back in his chair, his long legs thrust out in front of him, his blue eyes assessing her, his mouth quirking in a wry grin. 'Well, well, what am I to make of this change of heart?'

'Just that I shall miss you when you move out.'

'That's easily settled,' he said smoothly. 'We don't have to part. You can come and live with me.' He drew her onto his lap, pulling her down into the inviting warmth of his body so that she was all too conscious of his strong thighs, his hard male chest and the arms that warmly circled her waist. She looked at him hazily, a strange languor spreading through her, her senses heightened by the sudden intimacy, and she felt no compulsion at all to move.

Even so, she shook her head and said reluctantly, 'It wouldn't work.'

'Why shouldn't it? You have to give the idea at least half a chance before you set your mind against it.'

He was very still, quietly watching her, and she studied him dreamily in return, wanting to go along with what he was saying, to throw caution to the winds, but hearing all the while that inner note of warning that persisted in her head.

If only she could let down her guard just for once. She wanted him so much, and it would be easy just to snuggle into his arms and let him soothe away her fears with his kisses. She loved every line of his rugged features, those slanting cheek-bones, his strong jaw. His mouth was beautifully shaped, so firm, and vibrantly male...and so close that their lips might almost touch... Had he moved closer? Or had she moved towards him?

'Mollie?' He murmured her name softly, and his hand lightly stroked her face, his thumb gently brushing the line of her mouth. 'Take a risk, just for once, for me.'

'I daren't.' Why had she gone and fallen in love with him? She shouldn't have let it happen, but she had been beguiled by him. Love had crept up on her somehow in a fleeting moment while her guard had been down.

He didn't love her, though, did he? He wasn't even offering her marriage. He had only asked her to go and live with him, and that left her emotions in tatters. How could things ever work out the way she wanted? She wanted safety, security, a love that would last a lifetime. A long, long lifetime. Perhaps she was searching for the impossible.

His mouth sought hers and a little whimpering sound broke in her throat. Against her will her mouth softened and her lips parted. A smouldering heat was beginning to build inside her, a slow burn that made her arch restlessly in his arms. It would take just one spark to ignite the flame…

'I want you,' he muttered. He kissed her fiercely, and the flames burst around her and threatened to burn out of control. She didn't know how to handle it. If she let it go on she would soon be engulfed in the wildfire blaze…

Hadn't she learned from bitter experience that fire of that kind should be avoided at all cost? It was all-consuming, and it left nothing but ashes in its wake.

She dragged her mouth from his and looked up at him, wide-eyed, searching for answers.

Sam studied her features, his gaze quizzical. 'It's all right, Mollie—'

'No, it isn't.' Her throat was achingly dry. How did she know that she could trust him with her heart? 'I'm scared, Sam,' she whispered. 'You were right about me, I am a coward. It's just that everything goes wrong for me and I don't know how to make it right.'

His lips brushed her cheek. 'Believe me, there's no reason for you to be afraid.'

Wasn't there? Why, then, was her heart racing, he breath hard to come by? Somehow, in some basic instinctive way, she sensed that she needed to ge away, that she was treading on dangerous ground and that staying here was reckless folly.

The phone started to ring, and she jumped nervously.

'Don't answer it,' Sam muttered. 'Didn't we manage to get a locum on call tonight?'

She almost succumbed to the temptation to stay in his arms, but the ringing was strident and she hastily tried to collect her scattered thoughts.

'No, we didn't. Anyway, what if it's the hospital— if it's anything to do with Uncle Robert?'

Sam grimaced, releasing her reluctantly, and she went to answer the call.

It was an emergency and she quickly wrote down the details and then went to fetch her bag.

'I'll go,' Sam said. 'You stay here in case there's any news.'

She grimaced. 'I can't. I'll have to go out. It's Mrs Turner, and she'll feel happier if I'm the one who goes along. She gets very nervous and upset.'

She went to fetch her coat. 'I'll probably be gone quite a while. Her husband says she's weak down one side, and he can't make any sense of what she's saying. It sounds like a stroke so I'll most likely have to admit her to hospital.'

In a way she was glad of the need to drive. It gave her a chance to calm down and get things into a better perspective. It had been an emotionally exhausting day so far, and she wasn't in a proper frame of mind to make decisions where Sam was concerned.

Mrs Turner was very frightened by what had happened to her, and Mollie spent some time with her and the family, explaining the care and attention that she would need over the coming weeks and possibly months. She was admitted to the stroke unit, and Mollie assured them that it was the best place possible for her to be.

When she had finished talking to Mrs Turner's family, she decided to drive to the hospital to look in on Robert. The ward was quiet, but the night nurse recognised her and invited her into the office for a chat and a cup of coffee.

'He's sleeping,' she said later, when Mollie went over to the bedside. 'I think it's best if he gets as much rest as he can.'

'I won't disturb him,' Mollie told her. 'I'll just sit with him for a while, and perhaps you could let him know that I stopped by.'

It was late when she finally went back to the cottage, and the place was in darkness. Sam wasn't in the house, and she felt an overwhelming sense of loss and disappointment because he hadn't stayed. But, then, why would he when all she had done had been to push him away?

Then she found his note on the kitchen table. 'Mollie, I had to go out. I may as well take the opportunity to move into the house this weekend. I'll see you at the surgery on Monday.'

It was cold, and somehow final, and it hurt.

When she saw him in Reception on Monday morning she said, 'You decided to move into your house on Saturday night, then? That was a change of heart, wasn't it? I thought you were going to leave it until later this week.'

'It worked out easier this way. I had to go out on

a call before you came back from seeing Mrs Turner, and I didn't want to disturb you when I'd finished because I knew it would be the early hours of the morning. My house was closer than yours so it seemed logical to spend the night there.'

Logical. What else had she expected? That he would come back and take her in his arms and drive all her fears away? Hardly, when she had told him it wouldn't work between them. She was being thoroughly contrary, and totally illogical, not knowing what it was that she wanted. Cross with herself, she went to her room and immersed herself in work.

Later, when she had seen the last patient out of the door, she took the opportunity to phone the hospital and find out how Robert was.

'He seems to be fighting back now,' the ward sister told her. 'His appetite is improving, and it looks as though some of his strength is returning, so we're pleased with the progress he's making. It's early days yet, of course, but all the signs are good.'

Mollie felt her heart give a little leap in her chest. 'Thank you, Sister. I know he's in good hands. Give him my love, and tell him I'll be along to visit this evening, will you?'

'I'll do that.'

Mollie gathered up her bundle of patients' notes and took them along to Reception, a pleased smile on her face.

'You look cheerful,' Sam observed when he came out of his room. 'Have I missed a visit from George Clooney, or do I take it that there's been some good news from the hospital?'

She laughed. 'Fool,' she murmured, then said happily, 'Nothing tremendous, but they think Uncle Robert's improving.'

'I'm glad for you, Mollie. That's great news.'

'It is. Perhaps when I go to visit they'll let me know how much longer they expect to keep him in there.'

'Not too long, I imagine, given the rapid turnover in hospital beds these days. Let's face it, women who've just given birth face getting turned out after six hours to make room for someone else, so what chance has someone who's merely ill?' His expression was wry, but Mollie found herself nodding in agreement.

'He'll probably be home by the weekend.'

Sam went with her to see him that evening. She asked the consultant, Dr Hastings, about the prospects for her uncle's return home, but he wasn't committing himself yet.

'He's still quite weak, and there's an associated pernicious anaemia which complicates things so we need to treat that as well. I checked with the laboratory, and the tests you had already ordered were useful in that regard.'

He gave her a reassuring smile. 'At least we've been able to take him off the drip now, and he can take oral steroids. When he does leave hospital, of course, he'll need to continue taking them and increase the dosage in times of infection or other illness.'

'I know. Thanks for all you've done.'

Mollie went back to the ward to Robert's bedside. Laura was there, putting some flowers in a vase, and Sam was leafing through a car magazine with Robert and talking about the new registration number that was just out. Robert was still very white-faced and thin, but he looked up and smiled at her as she approached the bed, and she took his hand and squeezed it gently.

'Are you feeling any better?'

'Much better, thanks, Mollie, especially now we can put a name to what's wrong with me. I can't say I shall be sorry to leave here, though,' he added in a low voice, looking around the ward. 'They walk in, carrying my notes, then whisk them away before I even get a look. They put charts at the end of the bed where I can't see them. They decide between them what treatment they're going to give me, and I feel like saying, Hey, I'm the doctor, I'll do the prescribing.'

Mollie laughed at the indignation on his face. 'Now that's a sure sign you're on the mend. I expect you drive them to distraction.'

'Just wait till I'm steady on my pins again—'

'They'll be throwing you out,' Sam said drily.

He drove Mollie back to the cottage later. 'He looked more like his old self, didn't he?' he murmured, taking off his jacket and hanging it over a chair in the living-room.

'He did.' She leaned against the doorjamb, thinking about the way things had turned out. 'It makes me feel as though I want to celebrate.'

He smiled. 'Because something's going right in your life for a change?'

'Yes, it is, isn't it? I felt as though I was carrying such a weight around with me these last few months.'

He moved towards her. 'There was never any need

for you to carry it alone, don't you know that?' He
studied her thoughtfully, trying to read the expression
in her wide, green eyes.

'It was my problem,' she said. 'It was something
I had to handle on my own.'

He shook his head. 'That's where you've been going wrong all along,' he murmured softly. His arms
slid warmly around her. 'You keep forgetting that
I'm here to share things with you. I even suggested
that you come and live with me so that we can be
closer, but you turned me down. When are you going
to give in and accept that I'm here for you?'

She looked up at him doubtfully. 'Are you? I need
to know that you're there for me alone, but then, over
these last few weeks, when I've seen you getting
closer to Laura I don't know what to think. How can
I trust my feelings any more?'

His head went back and he studied her, a puzzled
expression on his face. 'Laura? What do you mean?'

Mollie fidgeted. 'You've been so close to her
lately, as though the pair of you were hiding something. What am I supposed to think?'

'I was trying to offer her support because she
wasn't feeling well. I helped her when she fainted
here one day, and I think she felt that she could trust
me enough to confide in me.'

She frowned, instantly concerned. 'What's wrong
with her?'

'Nothing. She's pregnant.'

She stared at him, open mouthed. 'What?'

'I said she's pregnant.'

'I heard what you said, I just can't take it in.' She
shook her head as though that would clear it. 'Why

didn't she tell me? She trusted you, yet she didn't feel she could share it with me.'

He grimaced. 'I more or less guessed. She'd been feeling nauseous and I just put two and two together. She was worried what your reaction might be. Most of all, she didn't want to hurt you. You and James had been engaged, and she didn't know how you would react to the fact that she was going to have his child. I think she was trying to find a way of breaking the news, but then her father was ill and it was the wrong time.'

His hands stroked her waist with slow, caressing movements. 'How do you feel about the news, Mollie?'

She drew in a shaky breath, trying not to think of what those hands were doing to her errant will-power. 'I'm glad for her, for them. I'm just surprised that she felt she couldn't tell me about it.'

She pulled a wry face. 'It felt strange at first, having them live close by. I was all right seeing Laura on a regular basis, but I wasn't sure how to get over the awkwardness that was bound to be there when I met James again. It was a difficult situation, and I felt too pressured with everything else that was going on here at home and at the surgery to be able to deal with it properly. I suppose that's why I wanted to put off going to the barbecue, just as I'd put off other events before.'

She looked up at him, her fingers twisting against the fabric of his shirt. She registered the warmth of his skin against her hands, felt the steady, reassuring thud of his heartbeat and wanted, more than any-thing, to run her fingers over his chest.

'I realised some time ago that I never really loved James properly, not in the way that he would have wanted. I think I do love him, but more like a brother. He was a good friend, he helped me through the bad times, and I really wish him the very best. I'm pleased for him and Laura that they're starting a family.'

Sam's breath caught in his throat, and he bent his head to her, his lips brushing her temple. 'I was so afraid that you had never got over him,' he muttered thickly, 'that there would be no room for me in your life.'

She lifted her hand to his face, tenderly stroking his cheek. 'There's always been room for you in my life,' she whispered. 'I was just so afraid. I daren't hope for something that might be snatched away from me at any moment.'

He crushed her softly to him, and his head bent towards her, his mouth seeking hers. He kissed her hungrily, possessively, and she clung to him, her body alight with a wild longing that only he could assuage.

'I love you, Mollie,' he said softly. 'I want to share everything with you. I want to wake up each morning and find you there, right next to me. Tell me that you want it, too?'

'Yes,' she whispered. 'It's what I want.'

'Will you marry me, then? Will you put your fears to one side and come and live with me, be with me for always? This time is forever, Mollie. We'll build a life together, we'll be happy, I know it, and we'll fill the house with our children. Just say you'll marry me.'

Her heart seemed to swell in her chest in a warm surge of joy. 'I will,' she said. 'Oh, yes...I will.' His arms tightened around her and his mouth claimed hers in a kiss that stirred a throbbing hunger in her body.

'Believe me,' he muttered against her lips, 'together we can overcome anything.'

She believed him. From now on she would live life to the full, rather than worry about what might happen tomorrow. A smile curved her lips. Somehow she sensed that from now on life was going to be everything her heart could wish for.

MILLS & BOON®

MEDICAL ROMANCE™

VINNING HER BACK by Lilian Darcy

Medicine and marriage, Southshore has it all

r Grace Gaines was devastated by the loss of her baby,
ore so as it became clear that her husband Marcus had not
anted the child. Their marriage under threat, Marcus had
ken a six month break, and now he was back. Would they
ay married or not…

JLES OF ENGAGEMENT by Jean Evans

ter her Uncle Jon suffers a heart attack, newly qualified
ctor Jamie agrees to act as a locum at his general practice.
n's partner, Dr Sam Paige, is not convinced she's up to the
. Her first priority is to prove herself and then make him
lise she's a woman too! But is she too late…

LLING FOR A STRANGER by Janet Ferguson

ward sister Anna Chancellor, returning to work after
t should have been her honeymoon was very hard.
g jilted made her feel she couldn't trust love again.
hopaedic Registrar Daniel Mackay's disastrous marriage
e him feel the same way. Can they dispense with
ion and accept the love they've found?

Available from 2nd June 2000

Available at most branches of WH Smith, Tesco,
Martins, Borders, Easons, Volume One/James Thin
and most good paperback bookshops

0005/03a

SAVING FACES by Abigail Gordon

As a teenager, Gemma Bartlett's face had been badly damaged in a car accident. Surgeon Jonas Parry had treate her and now, ten years later, she has become his junior doctor. Still in love with him after all these years, can she convince him that her feelings are genuine?

FOR PERSONAL REASONS by Leah Martyn

Dr Erika Somers needed time to consider her future and accepting a job as a locum for Dr Noah Jameson at Hillcre is ideal. Although on leave, Noah keeps coming back to h her and finally lets himself believe she will stay. But will their growing love be enough to keep her at Hillcrest?

LOVE ME by Meredith Webber
Book Two of a trilogy

When Dr Andrew Kendall returns from leave, he is immediately attracted to nurse Jessica Chapman. But Jes badly needs to know who her father is, and only her grandmother, Mrs Cochrane, can help. Before Jessica ca reveal who she is, Mrs Cochrane dies in suspicious circumstances. Suddenly, Jessica is unable to tell Andrew true story...

Puzzles to unravel, to find love

Available from 2nd June 2000

MILLS & BOON®

STRANGERS IN PARADISE

Meet Carrie, Jo, Pam and Angel…
Four women, each about to meet a
sexy stranger…
Enjoy the passion-filled nights
and long, sensual days…

Four stories in one collection

Not in My Bed!
by Kate Hoffmann

With a Stetson and a Smile
by Vicki Lewis Thompson

Wife is 4-Letter Word
by Stephanie Bond

Beguiled
by Lori Foster

Published 19th May

FREE!

4 Books
and a surprise gift!

We would like to take this opportunity to thank you for reading this Mills & Boon® book by offering you the chance to take FOUR more specially selected titles from the Medical Romance™ series absolutely FREE! We're also making this offer to introduce you to the benefits of the Reader Service™ —

- ★ FREE home delivery
- ★ FREE gifts and competitions
- ★ FREE monthly Newsletter
- ★ Books available before they're in the shops
- ★ Exclusive Reader Service discounts

Accepting these FREE books and gift places you under no obligation to buy; you may cancel at any time, even after receiving your free shipment. Simply complete your details below and return the entire page to the address below. **You don't even need a stamp!**

YES! Please send me 4 free Medical Romance books and a surprise gift. I understand that unless you hear from me, I will receive 6 superb new titles every month for just £2.40 each, postage and packing free. I am under no obligation to purchase any books and may cancel my subscription at any time. The free books and gift will be mine to keep in any case.

MOEB

Mrs/Miss/Mr ....Initials ....
BLOCK CAPITALS PLEASE

Surname ....

Address ....

....

....Postcode ....

Send this whole page to:
The Reader Service, FREEPOST CN8I, Croydon, CR9 3WZ
EIRE: The Reader Service, PO Box 4546, Kilcock, County Kildare (stamp required)

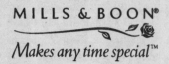